Welcome to the Asylum

Asylum Duet, Volume 1

Ashley Marie

Published by Ashley Marie, 2025.

WELCOME TO THE ASYLUM

First edition. January 17, 2025.

ISBN: 979-8230157878

Written by Ashley Marie.

Table of Contents

Dedication

I would like to thank my Edit Team: Jor Young, Hailey Mason and Elise Ballard for going out of your way and helping pinpoint some of the most funniest mistakes. Ladies you are the reason we are getting the ARCs out ahead of the release date.

I would like to thank my PA, Elise Ballard - Dream Weaver Services, I would be lost and a chaotic mess without you. You go above and behind to help me. Thank-you for everything. Thank-you for the friendship we have gained through every step of the way.

I want to thank my entire ARC for everything they do. I wouldn't be where I am at today without each and everyone of you.

I want to thank my Street Team: Micki-d Rawling, Jor Young, Shannon Oneil, Sefanie Silvestri, Alyssa Boyd, Elise Ballard, Joy-Anne Jorgensen.

I want to thank my Alpha Team: Haley K., Alyss Boyd, Michelle S., Amanda Myers, Joy-Anne Jorgensen, Amanda Felton, and Chelsea Kohutek for being badass and reading through this book and helping with everything in such a quick time-frame. You ladies are the best.

Triggers

Suicide
Violence
Death
Sexual Assault
Torture
Self-Harm
Psychological Horror/Disturbing Themes
Gore/Violence
Abuse/Manipulation
Unreliable timeline/narrator-due to the abuse inflicted on the FMC mind.

Synopsis

Welcome to the Crossroads Insane Asylum, where a dark past lingers in every crumbling brick. Here, you will discover the story of Abigale and the events that unfolded around her, along with the eccentric methods of Dr. Harker. Are you prepared to descend into madness like those who came before you? If the answer is yes, please enter at your own risk!

Intro

The flickering fluorescent lights cast a sickly pallor over the asylum's corridors, transforming shadows into grotesque specters that dance along the peeling wallpaper. I clutch my small bag of belongings to my chest, my knuckles bone-white with tension as I trail behind the stern-faced nurse. Her starched uniform rustles with each brisk step, the sound grating against my frayed nerves.

"Keep up," she barks over her shoulder, her voice as cold and sterile as the linoleum beneath our feet.

I quicken my pace, my heart pounds a frantic rhythm against my rib cage. The endless corridor before us is like a maze of hopelessness and broken spirits. As we go by a series of grimy windows, I catch glimpses of the world beyond—a world that now feels as distant and unreachable as the stars.

"Where exactly are you taking me?" I ask, my voice barely above a whisper.

The nurse doesn't turn around. "To your new home, Miss Sheetz. I suggest you get comfortable with the idea."

Home. The word echoes in my mind, a cruel mockery of everything I've lost. Sounds of muffled sobs and incoherent mutterings make me feel far from home.

We round a corner, and I freeze. A group of patients, their eyes vacant, huddle in an alcove, staring at a point in the middle distance. One woman, her hair a tangled mess, rocks back and forth, lips moving in a silent litany. Another man, rail-thin and trembling, presses himself against the wall as if melding with the crumbling plaster.

"Don't stare," the nurse hisses, grabbing my arm. "It's rude."

But I can't look away. In their hollow gazes, I see a reflection of my fears, my own potential future. Will I become like them, lost in the labyrinth of my mind?

As we pass, one patient turns to me, his rheumy eyes suddenly sharp with clarity. "The shadows," he whispers urgently. "They speak. Can you hear them?"

A chill races down my spine, leaving goosebumps in its wake. I open my mouth to respond, but the nurse's iron grip on my arm tightens painfully.

"Ignore him," she snaps. "Half the time, they don't even know what they're saying."

But as we continue down the corridor, leaving the group behind, I can't help but suspect they know more than anyone gives them credit for. The shadows here appear to have a life of their own, contorting and twisting in a way that defies explanation.

My thin sweater offers little comfort as I shiver, pulling it closer. "It's freezing in here," I murmur, more to myself than to my stern companion.

The nurse's laugh is devoid of warmth. "Oh, you'll get used to it. The cold is the least of your worries in this place."

Her words hang heavy with unspoken threats. The deeper we venture into Crossroads Insane Asylum, the more I fear the unspeakable things that may hide in its shadowy halls. Will I find salvation here, or will this be the place where my sanity finally shatters beyond repair?

A deafening crash shatters the eerie silence, echoing through the corridor like a gunshot. I leap backward, my heart hammering against my ribs. "What was that?" I gasp, my eyes darting wildly from door to door.

The nurse's nails digging into my flesh. "Just another patient having an episode," she says dismissively, but I catch a flicker of unease in her eyes. "Nothing to concern yourself with."

I'm not convinced. The crash was unlike any other. Deliberate. As if something were breaking free. "Are you sure?" I press, my voice trembling. "It sounded like—"

"I said it's nothing," the nurse snaps, yanking me forward. But I can't escape the impression that something is amiss, pervasive in the air, dense as fog and equally stifling.

We approach a heavy metal door at the end of the hallway. The nurse fumbles with a ring of keys, each clink sending a jolt of apprehension through my body. "Is this...is this where I'll be staying?" I ask, hating how small my voice sounds.

The lock finally gives way with a resounding clank. As the door creaks open, revealing a cramped, desolate room beyond with the smell of death, the nurse's lips curl into a stiff smile. "Welcome home, Abigale."

Chapter One

I step inside, my eyes darting from face to face. Some patients sit motionless, their gazes fixed on unseen points in space. Other's pace frantically, muttering incomprehensible phrases. A woman in the corner rocks back and forth, her arms wrapped tightly around her knees.

"This can't be real," I whisper, more to myself than anyone else.

A man shuffles past me, his eyes meeting mine for a moment. In that fleeting connection, I see a reflection of my own terror.

"You'll get used to it," he mumbles, his words barely audible.

My heart plummets. Get used to it? The thought of this becoming my norm sends a wave of nausea through me. I am about to retreat when a hush falls over the room.

Dr. Everett strides in, his tall frame casting a long shadow across the scuffed linoleum. His presence sucks the air from the room. As his gaze sweeps across the gathered patients, I shrink myself along, willing myself to become invisible.

But it's futile. His eyes lock onto mine, and for a moment, time stands still. There's something in his look–curiosity? Anticipation? — that makes my skin crawl. Just as quickly, he moves on, but the chill of his attention lingers.

"What does he want?" My mind is racing. "Why am I here? What are they going to do to me?"

The questions swirl in my head, each more terrifying than the last. As Dr. Everett speaks, his voice clinical and detached, I can't shake the feeling that I've stepped into a nightmare from which there may be no awakening.

Dr. Everett's voice cuts through the silence like a scalpel. "Miss Sheetz, come with me." His words are a command, not a request.

My legs tremble as I stand, every instinct screaming at me to run. But where? The asylum's maze-like corridors offer no escape. I follow him, my bare feet padding against the cold floor, each step carrying me deeper into the unknown.

"Where are we going?" I ask, my voice barely above a whisper.

He doesn't answer, just leads me down a dimly lit hallway. The walls seem to close in, the peeling wallpaper writhing like living things in the corners of my vision.

We stop at a heavy metal door. Dr. Everett produces a key, the lock clicks echoing ominously. "In here," he says, gesturing into the pitch-black room beyond.

My heart hammers against my ribs. "I... I don't want to go in there."

"It's part of your treatment, Miss Sheetz. Don't you want to get better?" His tone is cold, clinical, devoid of empathy.

I step inside, my breath catching in my throat as darkness envelops me. The door slams shut behind me, the lock engaging with a final, terrible click.

"Hello?" I call out, my voice swallowed by the absolute blackness. No response.

Panic rises in my chest. I fumble in the dark, hands outstretched, searching for walls, for anything solid to anchor me. There's nothing but space and the sound of my own ragged breathing.

"This isn't right," I cry out in my head while fighting to keep my composure.

Time loses all meaning in this lightless void. Minutes stretch into hours, or is it days? My mind fragments, memories, and fears, blending into a nightmarish tapestry.

"Help me," I whimper, but the darkness offers no solace. Instead, it seems to whisper back, echoing my deepest fears. I hear my mother's voice, disappointed and cold. My father's angry shouts. The mocking laughter of classmates.

"No one's coming for you, Abigale," the darkness hisses. "You're all alone here. Forever."

I curl into a ball on the floor, attempting to shut out the voices, but they only grow louder. "This isn't real," I tell myself, but doubt creeps in. What if this is my reality now? What if I never see the light again?

As I teeter on the edge of sanity, a chilling thought surfaces: What if Dr. Everett isn't curing me at all? What if he's breaking me?

Suddenly, a blinding light floods the room, searing my retinas. I cry out, shielding my eyes with trembling hands.

"Fascinating," Dr. Everett's cold voice cuts through the silence. "Your resilience is...unexpected."

I blink rapidly, focusing on his looming figure. "Please," I croak, my voice raw from disuse. "I can't take anymore."

He crouches beside me, his clinical gaze dissecting my every reaction. "But we've only just begun, Abigale. Your mind holds such potential."

A sharp prick in my arm makes me flinch. "What are you—"

"A little cocktail to heighten your senses," he explains, his tone gleeful. "We're pushing boundaries here, unlocking the secrets of the mind."

The room spins, colors bleeding into one another before I'm falling.

"Focus, Abigale," Dr. Everett's voice echoes, distorted. "Tell me what you see."

Visions assault me—fractured memories, nightmarish specters. I see myself as a child, alone and afraid. Then I'm running through Crossroads' twisted corridors, pursued by unseen horrors.

"I... I can't..." I gasp, overwhelmed by the onslaught.

"You can," he insists. "Your mind is the key. Breakthrough."

For a moment, clarity strikes. I see beyond the asylum walls, a glimpse of a world beyond this nightmare. But then darkness creeps in again, dragging me back into confusion and terror.

"No!" I scream, clawing at the air. "Let me out!"

But there's no escape from the labyrinth of my mind.

The darkness swallows me whole, a living entity that writhes and pulses around my fragile form. I curl into myself, feeling the cold floor beneath me, the only tangible reality in this void.

"Who are you?" The whisper slithers through the blackness, its source indiscernible.

"I'm... Abigale," I respond, my voice trembling. "Abigale Sheetz."

A chorus of laughter erupts, mocking and cruel. "Are you sure?"

Doubt creeps in, insidious tendrils wrapping around my thoughts. Who am I? The question echoes in the emptiness, reverberating through my fractured psyche.

"I don't... I can't remember," I whimper, pressing my palms against my temples.

The darkness shifts, revealing fleeting images—a young girl with curious blue eyes, a teenager screaming as she's dragged into Crossroads, a woman staring vacantly at peeling wallpaper. Are they all me? Or figments of a broken mind?

"Please," I beg, unsure who I'm addressing. "I need to get out. I need to find myself again."

"But darling," the darkness purrs, "you've always been here with us."

I struggle to my feet, staggering. "No. That's not true. I had a life before this. I had..."

The words die on my lips. What did I have? Family? Friends? The memories slip away like smoke, leaving only hollow echoes.

"You're ours now, Abigale," the voices whisper in unison. "Forever and always."

A spark of defiance ignites, causing me to clench my fists. "I'll find a way out, even if I have to tear this place apart with my bare hands."

The darkness laughs again, but this time, I detect a hint of unease. "Bold words for a shattered mind."

"I am broken," I snarl, "but I'm not defeated. Not yet."

As if in response, a distant light flickers—faint but unmistakable. Hope, fragile and desperate, blooms in my chest.

"I'm coming home." I murmur, taking a shaky step toward the light.

Chapter Two

The feeling of being pulled against my will into the unknown is not just overwhelming but consumes every inch of my consciousness. It is a terrifying dance in the darkness, spinning and twirling in the depths of the abyss.

I am nothing more than a puppet, my strings controlled by ghostly hands that remain hidden, their intentions unknown. They drag me relentlessly through a winding labyrinth of corridors, each turn leaving me dizzier and more disoriented than the last. The air is thick with fear and uncertainty, my heart racing as I am led deeper into the unknown depths.

My senses are my only connection to this harsh reality, and they are mercilessly assaulted. The frigid, damp stone beneath my bare feet feels like a violation, piercing through my skin with its icy touch. With each step, the cold creeps deeper into my bones, threatening to freeze me in place. Every breath I take is a struggle against the bitter chill that gnaws at my lungs. My body trembles uncontrollably as I press forward, determined to survive in this unforgiving environment.

I am lost in this abyss of darkness, unable to see beyond the reach of my own outstretched hand. It's as if a voracious beast, leaving nothing but an endless void in its wake, has devoured the world. The only glimmer of hope comes from flickering light bulbs scattered throughout; their weak glow barely strong enough to push back against the blackness.

In this eerie environment, even my breath feels foreign and unsettling as it hangs in the air like a tangible entity. I am a prisoner in this waking nightmare, at the mercy of the sinister forces that haunt this desolate place.

The distant echoes of screams and cries ricochet off the stone walls, reaching my ears as haunting reminders of my grim reality. Each sound is a symphony of despair, its discordant notes striking terror into my already trembling heart. These are the voices of other patients ensnared within this hellish institution, stating their fear and hopelessness, adding another layer to the unbearable weight pressing down on my psyche.

A towering, rusted behemoth looms before me—the ominous doorway to what they call the treatment room. Its surface is a patchwork of scratch marks and etchings, a morbid tapestry that tells the story of its grim past. Scrawled across its surface are the names of patients, long gone and forgotten, in a desperate plea for mercy. Their voices silenced, their fates sealed within the confines of this formidable facade.

Stepping into the room, I am greeted by an onslaught of sights and sounds that send shivers down my spine. The walls hum and buzz with electricity, like a malevolent orchestra tuning its instruments for a performance of terror. Each note is like a conductor's baton, directing icy tendrils of fear slithering down my spine. It is a symphony of impending doom, each crescendo heralding a fresh wave of dread and despair. This chamber of horrors is a suffocating nightmare, leaving me trapped with no escape.

The room is a cage, filled with the overpowering stench of antiseptic and something far more sinister. The sharp, chemical smell mingles with a faint, lingering odor of burnt flesh, creating a volatile blend that twists my stomach into knots and threatens to choke me. This unholy matrimony of scents is a ghastly reminder of the gruesome fate that awaits me.

As my eyes slowly adjust to the dim light, I am met with a macabre sight. This institution's relentless torture adorns with grotesque and horrifying images, each one a chilling masterpiece crafted by deranged minds pushed beyond their breaking points on the walls and ceilings. Their twisted forms seem to writhe and contort in my vision, their haunting presence threatening to unravel my sanity at any moment.

The cold, solid surface of the steel table beneath me is a cruel master, holding me down with its unyielding grip as I writhe in agony. My skin screams against the tight restraints, the unforgiving metal biting into my flesh like a savage predator. The air is thick and heavy with the stench of death that clings to every inch of this sterile chamber. The acrid smell of bleach only adds to the terror, making it difficult to breathe.

Every sound reverberates off the stark white walls, amplifying the cacophony of terror that fills this hellish place. Each echo is like a cruel taunt, a mocking reminder of my helpless state within this nightmarish contraption. The walls seem to tower over me, enclosing me in their unyielding grip as I am held captive within this endless maze of torment and fear. My heart pounds frantically, the beat echoing off the cold surfaces around me, a constant reminder of my desperation and longing for escape. This prison seems to feed on my fears, feeding them back to me in an unending cycle of torment and despair.

The cruel gag muffles my desperate screams, rendering them into pitiful whimpers that are drowned out by the deafening roar of machinery. The metal contraption constricts around my skull like a merciless vice, digging its sharp edges into my temples and relentlessly squeezing tighter with each passing second. As the pain intensifies, so does my terror—the fear of losing myself in this agonizing torment, the fear of being trapped here forever in a never-ending cycle of agony.

And then it begins.

A jolt of electricity surges through me like a raging river, searing through my physical body and piercing my very soul. It feels as if I am being torn apart from the inside out, a relentless pain that shows no mercy. In those excruciating moments before oblivion consumes me, I am struck with a terrifying realization—this is not a mere scientific procedure or medical experiment. It is a dark ritual, an offering of two ancient beings far beyond human comprehension. They have chosen me as their unwilling sacrifice, condemning me to an eternity of torment and enslavement in their twisted realm. The air itself seems to tremble with their presence as I succumb to their unfathomable power.

Chapter Three

Dark. Oppressive. Suffocating. Dark. My eyes flutter open, but the inky blackness remains impenetrable. Where am I? The last fragments of a nightmare cling to my consciousness, blurring the line between sleep and waking.

"Hello?" My voice emerges as a hoarse whisper, swallowed by the void. No response. Just the thunderous pounding of my heart and head from whatever they did to me.

I reach out, my trembling fingers seeking purchase in the darkness. Cold, rough stone meets my touch. A wall? I press my palm against it, using it as an anchor as I struggle to my feet.

"Is anyone there?" I call again, louder this time. The words echo and fade, leaving only silence in their wake.

Keeping one hand on the wall, I shuffle forward. My bare feet scrape against the gritty floor. Each step is tentative, fear of the unknown paralyzing my movements.

Where am I? The question loops endlessly in my mind. Flashes of memory tease at the edges of my consciousness—stark white corridors, the acrid smell of disinfectant, muffled screams. Crossroads. The name surfaces unbidden, sending a chill down my spine.

"No," I mutter, shaking my head to dispel the images. "Not there. Not again."

My questing hand encounters space where the wall should be. An opening? Hope flares in my chest, quickly extinguished as my fingers brush against cold metal bars.

"A cell," I whisper, the realization settling like lead in my stomach. "I'm in a cell."

Panic claws at my throat, threatening to overwhelm me. I force it down, gritting my teeth. I've survived worse. Not only that, but I will survive this.

I continue my exploration, trailing my hand along the bars until I reach another wall. As I feel my way around the perimeter, a memory surfaces—a tiny flashlight secreted away in the hem of my asylum-issued gown.

With shaking hands, I fumble at the coarse fabric. There! My fingers close around the small cylinder. I click the button, and a thin beam of light pierces the darkness.

For a moment, elation sweeps through me. Then I see the words scratched into the wall, illuminated by the meager light:

"WELCOME HOME, ABIGALE,"

The flashlight slips from my nerveless fingers, plunging me once more into darkness.

My heart pounds against my ribs like a caged beast, each frantic beat echoing in the silence. The darkness presses in, a tangible weight crushing the air from my lungs. I gasp, desperate for oxygen, but the stale air only fuels my mounting terror.

"Help!" I cry out, my voice cracking. "Is anyone there? Please!"

The words bounce off unseen walls, returning to mock me with their futility. I strain my ears, hoping for any response—a footstep, a whisper, anything to prove I'm not alone in this void.

Nothing.

"I shouldn't be here," I whisper, more to myself than any potential listener. "This isn't right. I was...I was..." But the memory slips away, lost in the swirling darkness of my mind.

I take a shuddering breath, centering myself. "Focus, Abi," I mutter. "You've been here before. You survived then. You'll survive now."

But doubt gnaws at the edges of my resolve. How long have I been here? Hours? Days? The darkness distorts time, stretching seconds into eternity.

"Hello?" I call again, louder this time. My voice echoes, hollow and desperate. "I know someone's out there. You can't just leave me here!"

Only silence answers. I sink to my knees, the cold floor seeping through the thin fabric of my gown.

"Please," I whisper, my voice breaking. "I can't...I can't do this again."

But there's no response, no reprieve. Just the endless dark, and the pounding of my heart.

A flicker in the corner of my eye startles me. I whip my head around, heart racing. "Who's there?" I demand, voice trembling.

Nothing.

But then—movement. A shadow, darker than the blackness surrounding me, darts across my vision. I scramble backward, my back hitting a wall. "No," I whisper. "You're not real. You can't be real."

The shadow lingers, its edges blurring and shifting. A whisper, so faint I could be imagining it, brushes against my ear. "Abigale..."

I clamp my hands over my ears. "Stop it!" I scream. "Leave me alone."

The whisper grows, multiplying into a chorus of unintelligible murmurs. I press my palms harder against my head, nails digging into my scalp. "This isn't happening," I mutter. "It's not real. It's not real."

My fingers brush against the rough wall behind me, and a desperate idea forms. I need to hold on to something tangible, something real. I turn, running my hands along the surface until I find a slightly protruding edge.

"One," I say aloud, dragging my fingernail across the wall. The pain grounds me, a sharp contrast to the ephemeral horrors surrounding me. "That's one day."

I continue, each scratch a defiant act against the darkness. "Two. Three. Four..."

The shadows dance at the edge of my vision, but I force myself to focus on the wall, on the growing tally of my imprisonment. It's the only reality I can trust now.

"How many days has it been?" I wonder aloud, my voice hoarse. "How long will they keep me here this time?"

The whispers surge, as if in response. I ignore them, continuing my count. It's all I have left to cling to in this endless night.

The lines on the wall blur together, a chaotic tapestry of time lost. I trace them with trembling fingers, trying to make sense of the jumbled marks. "One, two...seven? No, that can't be right." My voice cracks, unfamiliar to my own ears. "Was it seventeen days? Or seventy?"

A cackle erupts from my throat, startling me. "Does it even matter anymore?"

I spin away from the wall, my thoughts scattering like leaves in a storm. "They're watching, always watching," I mutter, eyes darting to the corners of the room. "The shadows have eyes, you know. They see everything."

"Abigale," a soft voice calls out. My heart leaps, desperate for connection.

"Hello? Is someone there?" I reach out, grasping at the darkness. "Please, I need help!"

Silence answers me once again, crushing, and absolute. The loneliness crashes over me in waves, threatening to drown me in its depths.

"I'm sorry," I whisper to the emptiness. "I didn't mean to upset you. Please come back." Tears stream down my face as I sink to the floor. "I'll be good, I promise. Just don't leave me alone again."

The darkness seems to pulse around me, alive with malevolent intent. I curl into myself, rocking back and forth. "I'm still here," I chant, voice barely audible. "I'm still Abigale. I'm still...me."

But even as the words leave my lips, I wonder if they're true anymore. Who am I in this void? What's left of the girl I used to be?

Chapter Four

A memory flickers—sunlight on my face, laughter in the air. But it feels like a dream, something that happened to someone else. The asylum has become my reality, its walls the boundaries of my existence.

"Is anyone out there?" I call out one last time, my voice echoing in the emptiness. "Please...I don't want to be alone anymore."

The darkness offers no solace, only the rasp of my breath and the fear of endless confinement.

My stomach gnaws at itself, a constant ache that has become my only companion. I cannot remember the last time I ate. Days? Weeks? Time has lost all meaning in this pitch-black void.

"Food," I rasp, my voice a brittle whisper. "Please...I need food."

I drag myself across the floor, bones protruding beneath paper-thin skin. My fingers, once nimble, now feel like twigs ready to snap. They scrape against the cold ground, searching for anything edible.

"There has to be something," I mutter, desperation clawing at my throat. "Anything."

A memory surfaces—the cruel orderly's laughter as he withheld my meals. "Freaks don't need to eat," he had sneered. Now, his words echo in my mind, taunting me.

"I'm not a freak," I whimper, but doubt creeps in. "Am I?"

The darkness presses closer, feeding on my insecurities. Shadows dance at the edges of my vision, taking shapes that mirror my deepest fears.

"No," I gasp, squeezing my eyes shut. "You're not real. You cannot hurt me."

But the voices start, a cacophony of whispers that grow louder with each passing moment.

"Worthless," they hiss. "Broken. Unwanted."

I curl into myself, attempting to block them out. "Stop it," I plead, my body trembling. "Leave me alone!"

The voices only grow stronger, feeding on my weakness. They remind me of every failure, every moment of doubt, every cruel word ever spoken to me.

"No one's coming for you," they taunt. "You'll die here, forgotten and alone."

I sob, my emaciated frame shaking with each breath. "That's not true," I whisper, but even I can hear the uncertainty in my voice.

The darkness laughs, a sound that chills me to my core. It knows it is winning, wearing down my last defenses.

"I am Abigale Sheetz," I say, clinging to the words like a lifeline. "I am strong. I will survive this."

But as hunger gnaws and fear consumes, I wonder how much longer I can hold on to hope in this unending night.

A sliver of light pierces the darkness, so suddenly it sears my retinas. I gasp, blinking rapidly as my eyes struggle to adjust. For a moment, just a fleeting instant, I see beyond this prison of shadows.

Sunlight streams through swaying trees. A gentle breeze carries the scent of grass and wildflowers. I am standing in a meadow, my bare feet sinking into soft earth. I inhale deeply, savoring the fresh air that fills my lungs.

"This is real," I whisper, my voice hoarse from disuse. "This is who I am."

Memories flood back—running through fields, laughing with friends, dreaming of a future full of possibilities. I remember the curiosity that once burned bright within me, the hunger to understand the world and my place in it.

"Abigale," a familiar voice calls. "Come inside, dinner's ready!"

Mom. The sound of her voice ignites a fierce longing in my chest.

"I'm coming!" I call back, but the words catch in my throat as the vision fades.

Darkness crashes over me like a tidal wave, threatening to drown me once more. But this time, something's different. A spark has been lit, a tiny flame of hope flickering in the void.

"No," I growl, clenching my fists. "I won't let you take this from me."

I push myself to my feet, ignoring the protest of weakened muscles. "I am Abigale Sheetz," I declare, my voice growing stronger with each word. "I don't belong here. I will find a way out."

My hands trace the walls, searching for any weakness, any sign of escape. "There has to be a door," I mutter. "They put me in here somehow. There must be a way out."

Exhaustion tugs at me, but I refuse to give in. "Keep moving," I command myself. "One step at a time. You can do this."

I stumble, catching myself against the rough stone. Blood trickles from my palm, but I barely notice the pain. "I will survive," I vow. "I will escape. And when I do, I'll make them pay for what they've done to me."

The darkness seems to recoil, as if sensing my newfound determination. For the first time in what feels like an eternity, I smile. It's a feral grin, full of teeth and promise.

"You hear that?" I shout into the void. "I'm coming for you. All of you. And when I'm done, Crossroads will be nothing but ashes."

The darkness presses in, suffocating, but I won't let it claim me. Not now. Not when I'm so close. My fingernails scrape against the wall, searching for any imperfection, any hint of an exit.

"There has to be a way," I rasp, my voice hoarse from disuse. "Think, Abi. Think,"

A memory flickers—a whisper of wind, a faint draft. Was it real, or just another trick of my fractured mind?

I pause, holding my breath. There it is again. A subtle current, barely perceptible, caressing my skin.

"Air," I whisper. "Air means there's an opening."

My heart races as I follow the elusive breeze, hands outstretched. Suddenly, my fingers brush against something different—a seam in the wall, almost imperceptible.

"This is it," I breathe, while tracing the outline of a hidden door. "But how do I open it?"

I press, push, and claw at the surface, desperation fueling my efforts. Nothing budges.

"No!" I scream, pounding my fists against the unyielding barrier. "Let me out!"

As if in response, a faint click echoes through the room. The wall shifts beneath my hands.

"It's opening," I gasp, disbelief and hope warring within me.

A sliver of sickly yellow light pierces the darkness, growing wider. The all too familiar stench of antiseptic and decay assaults my nostrils.

I hesitate at the threshold as terror and exhilaration battle for dominance. What horrors await me beyond this room? Can I face what lies ahead?

"I have to," I whisper, steeling myself. "It's the only way."

Taking a deep breath, I step forward into the commons, leaving the pitch-black room behind. The door closes behind me with a resounding thud, sealing my fate.

Chapter Five

I press myself against the cold wall, my heart pounding in my chest as I watch Nurse Ratched make her rounds. Her shoes click-clack down the hallway, a metronome of misery in this hellish place.

"Time for meds," she barks, her voice grating against my eardrums.

I shuffle forward with the other patients, keeping my head down as I accept the little paper cup filled with multicolored pills. The bitter taste floods my mouth as I swallow, but I've learned to hide the capsules under my tongue. Later, I'll spit them out and flush them away. I can't risk dulling my senses, not when freedom is so close I can almost taste it.

As we're herded back to our rooms, I strain my ears to catch snippets of whispered conversations.

"Did you hear about what happened in the East Wing?" a trembling voice murmurs.

"Shh! They'll hear you," another hisses back.

My curiosity piqued, I linger near their huddled forms, pretending to study a crack in the wall.

"They say screams echo through the night," the first voice continues. "Patients disappearing without a trace."

A chill runs down my spine. What horrors lurk in the shadows of this asylum? I need to know more if I'm going to escape this nightmare.

Back in my room, I curl up on my thin mattress, mind racing. The walls seem to close in around me, whispering dark secrets. I press my palms against my temples, trying to quiet the cacophony of voices that plague me.

"Focus, Abigale," I mutter to myself.

I force myself to breathe deeply, calming the storm raging within. As night falls, I lie awake, listening to the rhythmic footsteps of the night staff. Their patterns etch themselves into my memory—a blueprint for freedom.

Tomorrow, I'll dig deeper. I'll pry open the cracks in this facade and expose the rot beneath. And then, I'll find a way out of this house of horrors, no matter the cost.

The flickering fluorescent lights cast a sickly glow as I shuffle down the corridor, eyes darting to catch every detail. A nurse rushes past, her shoes squeaking on the linoleum. I freeze, back pressed against the wall, heart thundering.

"Where's Dr. Simmons?" she calls to an orderly. "We need him in Ward C, stat!"

"He's on break," the orderly replies, frustration clear. "Won't be back for another fifteen."

My pulse quickens. A distraction. An opportunity.

I slip into an empty room, mind racing. Fifteen minutes. What can I accomplish in fifteen minutes?

The room's lone window offers a tantalizing glimpse of freedom. I press my face to the glass, drinking in the sight of gnarled trees and mist-shrouded grounds. My fingers trace the outline of the building, memorizing its contours.

"Soon," I whisper. "I'll be out there soon."

A distant scream jolts me back to reality. I turn, scanning the room for anything useful. My gaze lands on a crumpled blueprint peeking out from beneath a stack of files.

"What have we here?" I murmur, carefully extracting the paper.

My hands tremble as I unfold it, revealing a maze of corridors and rooms. It's incomplete, torn at the edges, but it's a start. I commit every line to memory, building a mental map of my prison.

"East Wing, West Wing," I mutter, tracing the paths with my finger. "But where's the way out?"

Footsteps approach. I hastily refold the blueprint, sliding it back into place. As I slip out of the room, a nurse rounds the corner.

"Abigale? What are you doing here?" she asks, suspicion clouding her features.

I force a vacant smile, channeling the disjointed thoughts that often plague me. "The walls," I say, voice dreamy. "They whisper secrets. Do you hear them too?"

The nurse's expression softens to pity. "Come on, let's get you back to your room."

As she leads me away, I cast one last glance at the room holding the blueprint. Another piece of the puzzle, waiting to be solved.

My escape draws nearer with each passing moment. And when I break free, I'll tear this place apart, brick by brick, exposing every dark secret hidden within its walls.

The common room hums with restless energy, a cacophony of muttered conversations and manic laughter. I scan the sea of broken minds, searching for a flicker of lucidity. That's when I spot him—a gaunt man with hollow eyes, sitting motionless in the corner.

I approach cautiously, my bare feet silent on the cold linoleum. "The shadows have eyes here," I whisper, sliding into the chair beside him. "Do you see them too?"

He turns, piercing me with a gaze far too sharp for this place. "Cameras," he murmurs. "In the corners, behind the vents. But they can't see everything."

My pulse quickens. "I'm Abigale," I say, leaning closer. "And you are?"

"Emmett," he replies, his voice barely audible. "You're planning something, aren't you? I can see it in your eyes."

I hesitate, weighing the risk. But something in his demeanor compels me to trust him. "Freedom," I breathe. "Do you know the way?"

Emmett's lips twitch in a ghost of a smile that matches his white hair and pale features. "I've been here longer than most. I know things—secrets buried in these walls."

As we talk, I feel the pieces of my plan clicking into place. Emmett's knowledge fills the gaps from my own observations. He tells me of blind spots in the surveillance, of corridors rarely patrolled.

"There," he whispers, nodding toward a corner of the room. "See how the camera doesn't quite reach that spot?"

I follow his gaze, noticing the slight angle of the device. A thrill runs through me as I realize he's right—there's a small area just out of its range.

"How many more?" I ask, my mind racing with possibilities.

Emmett leans in, his breath hot against my ear. "Enough to make a difference if you're clever. But be careful, Abigale. This place doesn't let go easily."

As we continue our hushed conversation, I can't shake the feeling that we're being watched. Not by the cameras or the staff, but by something older, something woven into the very fabric of Crossroads Asylum.

I shudder, pushing the thought aside. It doesn't matter. Whatever malevolence lurks here, I'll face it head-on. Because now, with Emmett's help, I have a chance. A real chance at escape.

Nothing will stand in my way, not the staff, the security measures, or even the asylum itself, in my pursuit of seizing it.

Chapter Six

The supply closet door creaks open, and I slip inside, my heart thundering against my ribs. Darkness envelops me as I fumble in my pocket for the makeshift lock pick—a bent paperclip pilfered from the nurse's station. My fingers tremble as I work the lock on the inner cabinet.

"Come on, come on," I mutter, sweat beading on my forehead.

A soft click, and the cabinet swings open. I grab what I need: a small flashlight, batteries, a handful of safety pins. Each item feels like a lifeline, a promise of freedom.

Footsteps echo down the hall. I freeze, barely daring to breathe.

"Anyone there?" a gruff voice calls out.

I press myself against the wall, willing the shadows to swallow me whole. The footsteps grow louder, then pause just outside the door. My pulse roars in my ears.

"Must be hearing things again," the orderly grumbles, and moves on.

I release a shaky breath, clutching my stolen treasures to my chest. As I emerge from the closet, the asylum seems to loom around me, its walls pressing in. But I won't let it intimidate me. Not anymore.

"You think you can keep me here?" I whisper into the empty corridor. "Watch me prove you wrong."

With newfound determination, I set out to assess the limits of my confinement. I ghost through the hallways, timing the patrols, noting every squeaky floorboard and rusty hinge. The asylum reveals its secrets to me, one by one.

In the rec room, I catch Emmett's eye. He nods imperceptibly, and I know it's time.

"Did you hear about the new doctor?" I shout, my voice carrying across the room. As intended, it draws the attention of both patients and staff.

While all eyes are on me, I discretely slip a note to another patient—a message to be passed along, another piece of my escape plan set in motion.

"I hear he's got some unconventional methods," I continue, weaving a tale of horror and intrigue that holds my audience captive.

As I speak, I'm acutely aware of my surroundings. The camera in the corner, the orderly by the door, the ticking clock on the wall. Each element was a potential obstacle, each now a known quantity in my mental map of Crossroads.

When I finish my story, leaving my listeners wide-eyed and whispering, I retreat to a quiet corner. My mind races, piecing together everything I've learned.

"Soon," I murmur to myself, running my fingers along the rough asylum wall. "Soon, I'll be free of this nightmare."

But even as hope blooms within me, a chill runs down my spine. For a moment, I swear I hear the asylum itself laughing—a low, menacing chuckle that echoes through its hollow halls.

The flickering fluorescent light above me hums incessantly, its erratic rhythm matching the frantic pace of my thoughts. I scan the room, my gaze settling on Nurse Eliza. Her kind eyes betray a weariness that goes beyond physical exhaustion. I've seen it before—the look of someone whose ideals have been crushed under the weight of this place's atmosphere.

"Nurse Eliza," I call out, my voice a carefully crafted blend of vulnerability and desperation. "Can I talk to you for a moment?"

As she approaches, I study her face, searching for signs of sympathy or distrust. "What is it, Abigale?" she asks, her tone softer than most of the staff here.

"I...I've been having these dreams," I begin, weaving truth and fiction. "About the experiments. About what they're doing to us here. It's not right, is it?"

Eliza's eyes widen, a flicker of concern crossing her features. "Abigale, I—"

A blood-curdling scream erupts from down the hall, cutting her off. We both turn towards the sound, and I see the color drain from Eliza's face.

"I have to go," she says hurriedly, but I catch her arm.

"Wait," I plead, my voice barely a whisper. "You know it's wrong. You can help us. Help me."

For a split second, I see the conflict in her eyes. Then she pulls away, rushing towards the source of the scream.

I'm left alone, the echoes of anguish reverberating through the asylum's hollow halls. The cries of my fellow patients—victims of this twisted institution—fill my ears, each wail a dagger to my heart.

My fists clench at my sides, nails digging into palms. "This has to end," my resolve hardening like steel. "I'm not just escaping for myself anymore. I must expose this place to save them all."

The weight of this realization settles over me, heavy yet oddly empowering. I close my eyes, allowing the sounds of suffering to fuel my determination. When I open them again, the world seems sharper, more focused.

"I'm coming for you," I whisper to the asylum itself, my voice barely audible over the cacophony of misery. "Your days of tormenting us are numbered."

As if in response, the lights flicker ominously, casting grotesque shadows across the walls. But I'm no longer afraid. I've seen the true face of horror in this place, and I'm ready to fight back.

The rusted bed spring creaks as I slide my hand beneath the mattress, fingers probing for the loose seam I've carefully widened over weeks. My heart pounds, a frantic drumbeat echoing the urgency of my mission. From this secret cache, I withdraw a stolen scalpel, its edge glinting malevolently in the dim light filtering through barred windows.

"Soon," I whisper to the blade, my confidant in this house of horrors. "Soon we'll carve our way to freedom."

I tuck the scalpel into the hem of my gown, the cold metal a comforting presence against my skin. My gaze darts to the door, ears straining for any sign of approaching footsteps. The corridor beyond remains silent, save for the distant moans of the damned.

Crossing to the cracked mirror, I stare at my reflection—a gaunt specter with eyes too large, too knowing. "You can do this, Abi," I tell myself, my voice barely audible. "You have to."

A sudden knock startles me. I whirl, pulse racing, as the door creaks open. Nurse Eliza, my reluctant ally, slips inside, her face a mask of nervous determination.

"It's time," she whispers, pressing a key card into my trembling hand. "The night shift's about to change. You have ten minutes before they realize I'm not at my post."

I nod, swallowing hard. "Thank you," I manage, the words catching in my throat.

Eliza's eyes soften momentarily. "Just be careful. And Abigale? If you make it out, tell them. Tell them everything."

As she turns to leave, I grab her arm. "Come with me," I plead, a desperate hope blooming in my chest.

She shakes her head, a sad smile playing at her lips. "I can't. But I can do some good here. For the others."

The door closes behind her with a soft click, leaving me alone with the weight of what's to come. I take a deep breath, steeling myself for the gauntlet ahead.

"Now or never," grasping the doorknob with white-knuckled intensity.

The corridor beyond stretches like the maw of some great beast, shadows writhing along the peeling wallpaper. Each step feels like an eternity, my bare feet silent on the cold tiles. The key card trembles in my grip as I approach the first security door, its red LED eye watching me accusingly.

"Please," I whisper, swiping the card anxiously. For a heart-stopping moment, nothing happens. Then, a soft beep, and the lock disengages.

I slip through with the scalpel, its reassuring weight against my thigh. The path to freedom lies ahead, a treacherous labyrinth of locked doors and watchful eyes. But I've mapped every turn, memorized every blind spot.

"I'm coming," not sure if I'm addressing the world beyond these walls or the twisted souls still trapped within. "Hold on. I'm coming."

"Not so fast, little lady. Where do you think you are going?" The night shift orderly demands as he grabs my arm painfully and drags me towards my room.

"I am lost." I gasp out as I look frantically around, but no one is near my room.

"Here is your room. Now stay put." He growls out as he tosses me inside and slams the door.

Chapter Seven

The door, a behemoth of rusted iron and age-old secrets, resonates with a series of thunderous thuds, reverberating through the room like the ominous beat of war drums. Each strike, a brutal assault on the metal barrier, sends shivers down my spine as the sound echoes chillingly in my skull. I'm ensnared in this chilly, shadow-drenched atmosphere, feeling my grip on sanity splintering and shattering into a million shards with every resonating crash against the door.

In this dire landscape of fear and anticipation, Dr. Harker's arrival does nothing to ease my dread; instead, it cements the gruesome reality of the nightmare I'm entrapped in. His footsteps resonate in the cold stone chamber, each echo adding a layer to the eerie symphony that seems to seep from within the very marrow of my bones. Confusion and terror shroud my thoughts, making it impossible to focus on anything beyond the sense of captivity that clings to me like a second skin.

His voice slices through the silence with the precision of a surgeon's blade, seeping with a malicious glee that turns my blood to ice. His words slither into my ears like venomous serpents, their hisses filling me with a primal instinct to flee. Yet, there is no escape from this icy purgatory he has ruthlessly thrown me into.

As he steps further into the room, his imposing figure casts an ominous shadow that swallows everything in its path. Harsh neon light from the hallway washes over Dr. Harker, his vacant, emotionless eyes, like bottomless pits, pierce into my soul.

"I...I was lost," I stammer, barely audible words tumbling from my trembling lips as I cower before his overwhelming menace. The air hangs heavy and suffocating around us, a macabre shroud of impending doom ready to consume me. Meeting his intense stare feels akin to staring into the abyss, surrendering to oblivion itself.

His laughter, cruel and devoid of mirth, slices through the silence like a death knell, sending tremors of dread down my spine and freezing my heart in my chest. It isn't merely a sound, but a living entity, a materialization of all my darkest fears.

The treatment room, sterile and uninviting, resembles a shrine dedicated to torment and suffering. The harsh fluorescent lighting casts an unforgiving glare on the metal surfaces that glint ominously, mirroring the icy grip of fear that holds me captive. At the room's center stands a monstrous machine—an unholy creation of metal and malice, promising unimaginable agony.

The chilling tank beckons to me, its thick crimson liquid swirling with sinister vines. The dim light casts eerie shadows that dance around the walls, creating a ghastly atmosphere. My heart beats wildly against my chest as I prepare myself for the horrors that await me.

Dr. Harker's experiments know no bounds; I am about to endure an unthinkably terrifying experience. As I am lowered into the icy tank, phantom chills seep into my bones, threatening to freeze me from the inside out. Fear and helplessness wash over me as I brace for what comes next.

Strong hands grip me tightly on each side and pull me towards a menacing machine, despite my screams and pleas for mercy. There is no escape from this place of horrors.

I am strapped down tightly, feeling the restraints dig mercilessly into my skin. The suffocating feeling of being trapped overwhelms me as I struggle against the bonds, desperate for freedom from this nightmare.

The imposing machine gleams mockingly in front of me, its metallic surface reflecting the terror in my eyes. With a flick of a switch, Dr. Harker unleashes a rush of frigid water into the chamber, numbing every inch of my body and rising higher with each passing moment. The icy embrace fills me with fear and paralyzes me in place.

But it's not just water that poses a threat in this cruel experiment. Blood-red vines line the walls, slithering closer with otherworldly energy pulsating through their sinewy bodies. They coil around me like serpents, squeezing and constricting until every inch of my body throbs with unimaginable pain. Each vine feels like a thousand needles piercing my skin, tormenting me beyond belief.

My screams echo off the cold, sterile walls, creating a symphony of raw agony. Dr. Harker looms over me with his sadistic grin, reveling in my suffering. He feeds off my pain, relishing in the power he holds over me.

Just as I reach the brink of endurance, the vines tighten their grip, crushing my chest and stealing every breath from my lungs. Waves of excruciating torture blur my vision and plunge my mind into darkness.

As I slip deeper into oblivion, the vines suddenly loosen their hold, granting a brief respite from the torment. Darkness envelops me, offering a small reprieve from the horrors inflicted by Dr. Harker.

But all too soon, blinding lights flood my vision once more, revealing Dr. Harker's grotesque form towering above me. My screams reach new heights as he cackles maniacally, relishing in his cruel experiments.

As I near certain death, everything fades into blackness—a merciful release from the endless cycle of torture and brief moments of relief in darkness. It is a welcome escape from the horrors inflicted by Dr. Harker's twisted mind.

Chapter Eight

Waking up with a painful gasp, the shadows writhe on the walls, mocking me. As I pace my cramped room, each step is a thunderclap in the suffocating silence. My mind races, replaying the horrors I've endured within these cursed walls. The electrodes. The ice baths. The screams—oh God, the screams.

"You're not real," I whisper, clawing at my scalp. "None of this is real."

But the peeling wallpaper and rusted bed frame tell me otherwise. This nightmare is my reality, has been for years. How many? I've lost count.

I whirl to face the grimy window, pressing my forehead against the cold glass. Beyond lies a sea of mist-shrouded trees, their gnarled branches reaching for me like skeletal fingers. No escape. No hope.

A memory surfaces—white-coated figures looming over me, voices dripping with false concern. "This is for your own good, Abigale. You're sick. We can help you."

"Liars!" I snarl, slamming my fist against the wall. Pain blooms, grounding me in the present. "You never wanted to help. You only wanted to break me."

My reflection stares back at me from the cracked mirror—a gaunt specter with wild eyes and tangled hair. I hardly recognize myself anymore. What have they done to me?

A floorboard creaks in the hallway, and I freeze. Footsteps. Coming closer. My heart pounds a frantic rhythm against my ribs as I strain to listen. Heavy. Measured. Purposeful.

"No," I breathe, backing away from the door. "Not again. Please, not again."

My senses sharpen to a knife's edge. I can hear the rustle of starched fabric, smell the acrid tang of antiseptic. My muscles coil, ready to fight or flee. But there's nowhere to run in this prison of the mind.

The footsteps halt outside my door. A key scrapes in the lock. I brace myself for whatever fresh hell awaits me, my nails digging crescents into my palms.

"Whatever you do to me, I won't break." I vow, my voice barely a whisper.

The door opens, and I steel myself to face the darkness that lies beyond.

The door swings open, and Dr. Alistair Harker's imposing figure fills the frame. His dark, unkempt hair falls across his forehead, partially obscuring eyes that seem to pierce through my very soul. I stumble backward, my breath catching in my throat.

"Miss Sheetz," he says, his voice a low, measured cadence that sends chills down my spine. "How fortuitous to find you awake."

I press myself against the far wall, my heart thundering. "What do you want?" I choke out, my voice trembling despite my efforts to steady it.

Dr. Harker steps into the room, closing the door behind him with a soft click that echoes like a gunshot in the silence. His gaze never leaves mine as he approaches, each step deliberate and predatory.

"I've been observing you, Abigale," he says, his tone almost caressing my name. "You're different from the others. Special."

My mind races, trying to decipher his words. Special? Is this another trick, another cruel experiment? I've learned to mistrust kindness in this place of shadows.

"Your case fascinates me," Dr. Harker continues, now mere feet away. "I believe you possess abilities beyond the ordinary. Abilities that, with proper guidance, could unlock the very secrets of the human mind."

I feel a flicker of something. Curiosity? Hope? No, I can't afford hope. Not here. Not now. "You're wrong," I whisper, but even as the words leave my lips, I'm not sure that I believe them.

Dr. Harker's lips curl into a smile that doesn't reach his eyes. "Am I? Tell me, Abigale, have you ever experienced moments of clarity? Visions that transcend time and space?"

My breath catches. How could he know? The fragments of shattered reality that sometimes invade my waking hours, the whispers of truths I can't quite grasp, I've never spoken of them to anyone.

"I... I don't know what you're talking about," I lie, but my voice wavers, betraying me.

"Oh, but I think you do," Dr. Harker says softly, his gaze intensifying. "And I can help you understand. To harness that power within you."

A part of me yearns to believe him, to grasp at this lifeline of understanding. But the scars of past betrayals run deep, and I can't shake the feeling that I'm standing on the precipice of something both wondrous and terrible.

"Why should I trust you?" I ask, my voice barely above a whisper.

Dr. Harker's smile widens, revealing teeth that seem too sharp in the dim light. "Because, my dear Abigale, I may be the only one who truly sees you for what you are. Not broken, but evolving. And I intend to nurture that evolution, no matter the cost."

His words hang in the air between us, laden with promise and threat in equal measure. As I meet his gaze, I realize that my world has shifted irrevocably. For better or for worse, nothing will ever be the same again.

I swallow hard, my throat dry as sandpaper. The weight of Dr. Harker's words presses down on me, suffocating yet oddly exhilarating. My fingers twitch, picking at the frayed edges of my sleeves as I struggle to find my voice.

"I... I see things," I finally whisper, the confession tumbling out like a secret long-buried. "Flashes of moments that haven't happened yet. Echoes of pain that aren't mine." I pause, my eyes darting to the shadows in the corners of the room, half-expecting them to lunge forward. "And sometimes, I hear the dead whispering."

Dr. Harker leans in, his eyes glittering with an intensity that both terrifies and captivates me. "Go on," he urges, his voice a silky caress.

"It's like being torn apart and stitched back together, over and over," I continue, my words spilling out faster now. "I can't control it. I can't make sense of it. It's driving me mad."

"Madness," Dr. Harker muses, his lips curling into a smile that doesn't reach his eyes, "is often a label for that which we don't yet understand. Your mind, Abigale, is not broken. It's evolving."

I shake my head in confusion. "But how? Why me?"

"The human mind is a labyrinth of untapped potential," he replies, his voice taking on a hypnotic quality. "Your experiences here have cracked open doors that most keep firmly shut. But to truly harness this gift, you must walk through the darkness."

A chill runs down my spine at his words. "And if I refuse?"

Chapter Nine

Dr. Harker's expression hardens for a moment, a fleeting glimpse of something cold and calculating. "Then you condemn yourself to a half-life, forever torn between two worlds, never truly belonging to either."

I feel the weight of his words settle over me like a shroud. The promise of understanding, of control, dangles before me like forbidden fruit. But the price feels steep, and I can't shake the feeling that I'm bargaining with something far beyond my comprehension.

My heart pounds, a frantic drumbeat echoing the chaos in my mind. I can't tear my gaze from Dr. Harker's piercing eyes, feeling as if he's peering into the very depths of my fractured psyche.

"What if..." I whisper, my voice trembling, "what if I lose myself completely? What if there's nothing left of me?"

Dr. Harker leans forward, his presence suddenly overwhelming. "My dear Abigale, it's not about losing yourself. It's about becoming who you were always meant to be."

I shudder, his words seeping into me like ice water. The allure of understanding, of harnessing this terrifying power within me, wars against the primal fear of shattering what little sanity I have left.

"I don't know if I'm strong enough," I confess, my fingers twisting anxiously in my lap.

A ghost of a smile flickers across Dr. Harker's face. "Strength isn't about being unbreakable, Abigale. It's about piecing yourself back together, stronger than before."

He reaches into his pocket, retrieving a small, gleaming object. "Here," he says, extending his hand. "A token of our connection, and of the potential I see in you."

In his palm rests a delicate silver pendant, its surface etched with intricate, swirling patterns that seem to shift and dance as I stare. At its center, a small, dark stone pulses with an otherworldly energy.

"What is it?" I breathe, unable to look away.

"A key," Dr. Harker murmurs, "to unlock the doors within your mind. Wear it and let it guide you through the labyrinth of your consciousness."

As I reach out to take it, my fingers trembling, I can't shake the feeling that I'm sealing a pact with the devil.

Dr. Harker's footsteps recede down the corridor, but his presence lingers like a phantom pressing against my skin. I clutch the pendant, its cool surface warming in my palm. My heart races, a caged bird desperate for flight.

"What have I done?" I whisper to the empty room, my voice trembling. The walls seem to lean in, listening.

I pace, my bare feet silent on the cold floor. Each step feels like a choice between two abysses—the familiar horrors of my fractured mind, or the unknown terrors of embracing these abilities.

"They're not abilities," I mutter, arguing with myself. "They're delusions. Madness."

But the weight of the pendant anchors me to a different reality. One where the impossible bleeds into the everyday, where the shadows whisper truths if only I'd listen.

I halt at the window, pressing my forehead against the cool glass. The asylum grounds stretch before me, a patchwork of overgrown gardens and crumbling outbuildings. Somewhere out there, answers lurk. Truths about myself, about this place, about the experiments that haunt my dreams.

"I have to know," I decide, my breath fogging the glass. "Even if it destroys me."

The pendant pulses against my skin as I slip it over my head. A jolt of electricity races down my spine, and for a moment, the world shimmers at the edges, reality bending like heat waves off summer pavement.

I steady myself against the windowsill, my legs suddenly weak. "Oh god," I gasp. "What am I becoming?"

But even as fear claws at my throat, a fierce determination rises to meet it. I've survived this long. I've endured torments that would have broken others. If there's a way to turn this curse into a weapon, to expose the rot at the heart of Crossroads, I'll find it.

"No more hiding," I vow to my reflection, a stranger with wild eyes staring back at me. "No more being a victim."

The asylum creaks and groans around me, as if sensing the shift in the air. I straighten my shoulders, feeling the weight of my decision settle over me like a shroud.

"I'm coming for you," I whisper into the shadows. "All of you."

I push open the door to my room, wincing at the shrill creak that echoes down the corridor. The sound awakens the very walls of Crossroads, and a thousand unseen eyes fall upon me as I step into the dimly lit hallway.

The flickering bulbs overhead cast a sickly yellow glow, transforming the peeling wallpaper into a living, writhing entity. Shadows dance and twist, forming grotesque shapes that seem to reach for me with grasping fingers.

"Stay calm," I mutter to myself, my voice barely audible over the pounding of my heart. "They're just shadows. Just tricks of the light."

But even as I speak, a chill runs down my spine. In this place, nothing is ever what it seems.

I force myself to move forward, each step a battle against the urge to flee back to the relative safety of my room. The floorboards creak beneath my feet, a symphony of decay that marks my progress through the asylum's labyrinthine corridors.

As I round a corner, a sudden gust of wind extinguishes several of the candles, plunging the hallway into near-darkness. I freeze, my breath catching in my throat as the shadows deepen and coalesce.

"Who's there?" I call out, my voice trembling despite my efforts to sound brave.

No answer comes, save for the faint whisper of unseen movement just beyond my field of vision. I press on, my fingertips trailing along the wall for guidance, feeling the raised patterns of mold and decay beneath my skin.

"You can do this, Abigale," I tell myself, summoning the determination I felt mere moments ago. "The hydrotherapy room holds answers. You need to know."

As if in response to my thoughts, a distant sound reaches my ears—the steady drip of water echoing from somewhere ahead. My pace quickens, drawn inexorably towards that haunting rhythm.

Finally, I round one last corner and there it is: the hydrotherapy room. The door looms before me, its paint peeling away in long strips like flayed skin. My hand hovers over the tarnished door knob, trembling with a mixture of fear and anticipation.

"Whatever's in there," I whisper, "I can face it. I must."

I wrap my fingers around the cold metal, feeling the weight of my decision. The asylum seems to hold its breath, waiting. With one final, shuddering exhale, I turn the knob, ready to confront the horrors that lie beyond.

Chapter Ten

My footsteps echo hollowly as I move forward, each creaking floorboard a warning of the horrors that lie ahead.

As I round a corner, a flicker of movement catches my eye. I freeze, pressing myself against the peeling wallpaper. Is it just a trick of the light, or something more sinister?

My mind races with possibilities, fragments of memories from my time as a patient here clashing against the present. I see myself strapped to a chair, needles piercing my skin as Dr. Everett looms over me with a cruel smile. I blink hard, forcing the vision away.

"Focus, Abigale," I mutter. "You're here for answers, not to lose yourself in the past."

I push on, my senses heightened to a painful degree. Every shadow seems to writhe with malevolent intent, every distant sound of a harbinger of discovery. My heart thunders in my chest, drowning out the whispers that seem to emanate from the very walls.

As I descend a narrow staircase, the temperature plummets. Goosebumps rise on my arms, and I wrap them tightly around myself.

"Hello?" I call out, immediately regretting the decision as my voice echoes back to me, distorted and mocking.

I reach the bottom of the stairs, finding myself in a long, dimly lit corridor. Water drips steadily from a rusted pipe overhead, the rhythmic sound like a twisted metronome counting down to some unspeakable revelation.

"This is where it happened," I murmur, fragments of memory coalescing into horrifying clarity. "This is where they broke us."

I take a tentative step forward, my foot squelching in a puddle of murky water. The sound triggers something within the asylum itself, and a low groan reverberates through the walls. I spin around, searching for the source, but find only more shadows and decay.

"I'm not afraid of you," I declare, my voice trembling despite my efforts to sound brave. "I've lived through your worst. Now it's time for the truth to come out."

As if in response, a chilly breeze caresses my cheek, carrying with it the faintest whisper of a name I'd long tried to forget. I shudder, pressing on into the darkness, my determination burning brighter than my fear. Whatever secrets Crossroads holds, I will uncover them, even if it means facing the demons of my past head-on.

My fingers trace the crumbling wallpaper, searching for any hidden irregularities. Suddenly, they catch on something—a slight protrusion behind a peeling section. With trembling hands, I pry it back, revealing a weathered bookshelf concealed within the wall.

"Of course," I whisper, a bitter laugh escaping my lips. "More secrets."

I run my hands along the dusty shelves, feeling for any mechanism or switch. A loose board shifts under my touch, and I hear a faint click. The bookshelf swings open, revealing a locked door behind it.

My heart races as I fumble through my pockets, searching for anything that, I think, will serve as a makeshift key. "Come on, come on," I mutter, frustration mounting.

Then, a memory flashes—a rusted key I'd pocketed earlier, thinking it insignificant. Could it be?

I retrieve it, my hands shaking so violently, I nearly drop it. "Please," I plead to no one and everyone, "let this be it."

The key slides in, and with a turn that feels like it takes an eternity, I hear the lock disengage. A wave of excitement and terror washes over me as I push the door open, revealing a small, dimly lit room beyond.

"What horrors are you hiding?" I ask the asylum, stepping inside. The air is thick with dust and the weight of forgotten suffering. Shelves line the walls, laden with artifacts that whisper dark secrets.

I approach a shelf, picking up a tarnished silver picture frame. The photograph inside shows a group of doctors, their smiles chilling in their false warmth. "You monsters," I snarl, recognizing one face in particular. "Dr. Everett, what did you do to us?"

Setting the frame down, I continue my search, my eyes darting from object to object. Each item seems to pulse with malevolent energy, a testament to the asylum's dark past. I pick up a leather-bound book, its pages yellowed with age.

"Show me," I demand, flipping it open. "Show me what they did here."

As I scan the pages, my vision blurs, memories threatening to overwhelm me. I clutch the book tighter, forcing myself to focus. My voice echoes in the small room as I tell the asylum, "I won't let him win." "I'll expose every twisted experiment, every broken soul. Your reign of terror ends now."

My breath catches as I flip through the journal, each page revealing more horrifying details of Dr. Everett's experiments. "Oh God," I whisper, my hands trembling. "They...they were breaking our minds."

Vivid descriptions of patients screaming, begging for mercy as they're subjected to ice baths and electroshock therapy assault my senses. I can hear their cries echoing through time. I'm filled with tears as I envision myself going through the same thing not that long ago.

"How could they do this?" I ask the empty room, my voice cracking. "We were people, not lab rats!"

A memory flashes — icy water, my own screams. I shake my head violently, pushing it away. "Focus, Abigale," I mutter. "You're here to uncover the truth."

As I set the journal down, my gaze falls on a large, cracked mirror leaning against the far wall. Something about its placement seems...off.

"What are you hiding?" I approach cautiously, studying my fractured reflection. My fingers trace the mirror's edge, feeling for any irregularities. Suddenly, I feel a slight give. "Gotcha."

With a soft click, the mirror swings open, revealing a dark passage beyond. A chill runs down my spine as I peer into the inky blackness.

"Well, Abi," I say to myself, steeling my nerves, "down the rabbit hole we go."

Taking a deep breath, I step through the opening, descending into the unknown. The darkness swallows me whole, and I can't shake the feeling that I'm walking straight into the asylum's twisted heart.

The darkness yields reluctantly as I fumble along the hidden passage, my fingers tracing the damp, uneven walls. A musty scent assaults my nostrils, reminding me of forgotten corners and buried secrets. As I emerge into a dimly lit room, my eyes widen in disbelief.

"O! shit," I whisper, my voice barely audible.

Row upon row of filing cabinets stretch before me, their metal surfaces dulled by years of neglect. This forgotten wing of the asylum holds the very essence of its dark history.

"What other nightmares are you hiding?" I mutter, approaching the nearest cabinet.

With trembling hands, I pull open a drawer. The scrape of metal on metal echoes ominously in the stillness. Inside, manila folders overflow with patient records, each one a testament to the suffering endured within these walls.

As I leaf through the files, all the names and faces blur together. But it's the notes—clinical, detached observations of human agony—that make my stomach churn.

"Subject exhibits extreme distress during treatment," I read aloud, my voice quavering. "Recommend increasing voltage for optimal results."

A wave of nausea washes over me. "Optimal results," I spit out. "Is that what they call our pain?"

My fingers brush against something glossy. Photographs. I pull them out, and immediately wish I hadn't. The images before me depict the old hydrotherapy room in nauseating detail—rusted tubs filled with murky water, restraints hanging ominously from the sides.

"I remember this. I remember..." I choke out, my legs threatening to give way.

A memory surfaces, the biting cold of the water, my own screams echoing off the tiled walls. I grip the edge of the cabinet, fighting to stay upright as the room spins around me.

"No," I grit out, forcing the memory back. "I won't let them win. Not now, never."

Chapter Eleven

With renewed determination, I continue my search. The truth is here, hidden in these files and photographs. And I'll find it, no matter the cost to my sanity.

"Dr. Everett," I mutter, rifling through more folders, "your secrets won't stay buried forever. I'll make sure of that."

My heart pounds as I leave the file room behind, driven by a desperate need to confront the horrors of my past. The corridor stretches before me, a dimly lit tunnel of lichen-covered stone and flickering shadows. Each step echoes, a haunting reminder of my solitude in this forsaken place.

At the end of the hallway, another heavy iron door looms. My breath catches as I recognize it from the photographs. "The hydrotherapy room," I whisper, my voice barely audible.

I retrieve the key from my pocket, its cold metal biting into my palm. "This is it," steeling myself. "The answers I need are behind this door."

With trembling hands, I insert the key. The lock resists, as if keeping its secrets. I grit my teeth, twisting harder. "Come on," I hiss, "open, damn you!"

A loud click reverberates through the hall. The door creaks open, revealing a chamber of nightmares.

"Oh fuck," I gasp, frozen on the threshold. The stench of rust and decay assaults me, carried on a frigid draft that penetrates my very bones.

I force myself to step inside, my eyes darting around the room. Rusted tubs line the walls, their surfaces pitted and scarred. Overhead, ancient pipes snake across the ceiling, dripping steadily into murky puddles on the cracked tile floor.

"I'm here," I announce to the empty room, my voice quavering. "I've come back."

The stillness is broken only by the rhythmic drip of water and the echo of my footsteps. Each sound seems amplified, as if the room itself is alive, watching, waiting.

"Show me," I demand of the shadows. "Show me what else has happened here."

But only silence answers, punctuated by the pounding of my heart.

I approach one of the rusted tubs, my heart hammering against my ribs. The metal is cold beneath my fingertips, its rough surface a testament to years of neglect and suffering. I hesitate, my hand hovering over the water within.

"Do it, Abigale," I whisper to myself. "Face your fears."

With a sharp intake of breath, I plunge my fingers into the icy water. The shock of cold sends a jolt through my entire body, memories flooding back in a torrent.

"No!" I gasp, yanking my hand back. "Not again, please."

But I force myself to stay, gripping the edge of the tub with white-knuckled determination. "I won't let you win," I growl, addressing the ghosts of my past. "I'm stronger now."

As I turn to explore further, the room seems to shift and warp around me. Shadows dance at the corners of my vision, teasing and taunting. I spin, trying to catch them, but they always remain just out of sight.

"Who's there?" I demand, my voice echoing off the walls.

A whisper responds, so faint I almost missed it. "Help us..."

"Who are you?" I ask, my eyes darting frantically around the room. "What happened to you?"

The temperature plummets, my breath visible in the suddenly frigid air. I wrap my arms around myself, shivering uncontrollably.

"This isn't real," I mutter, trying to convince myself. "It's just my mind playing tricks."

But the whispers grow louder, a cacophony of tormented souls crying out for release. I clamp my hands over my ears, but their voices penetrate my skull.

"Stop!" I scream, falling to my knees. "Please, just stop!"

The room spins around me, reality blurring at the edges. I fight to maintain my grip on sanity, clawing desperately at the fragments of my fractured mind.

"I won't let you break me," I growl through gritted teeth. "I've come too far to give up now."

As I struggle to my feet, my eyes lock onto a peculiar seam in the floor beneath one of the rusted tubs. With trembling fingers, I trace its outline, feeling a subtle give beneath my touch. My heart races as I pry at the edge, revealing a hidden compartment.

"What secrets do you hold?" I whisper, my voice barely audible over the persistent whispers that fill the room.

I reach inside, withdrawing a collection of personal effects. A tattered doll with button eyes that seem to follow my movements. A leather-bound journal with pages yellowed with age. A locket, tarnished and cold against my palm.

As I open the locket, a faded photograph falls out. A young woman's face stares back at me, her eyes haunted by unspoken horrors.

"Who were you?" I ask, running my thumb over the image. "What did they do to you here?"

The whispers intensify, as if in response to my questions. I flip open the journal, my eyes widening as I read the first entry:

"Day 1: They say this place will cure me. But I've seen the doctor's eyes. There's no healing here, only pain."

"Day 2: The treatments have begun. The icy water chills me to the bone, but it's nothing compared to the coldness in Dr. Everett's gaze. He watches me with a hunger that makes my skin crawl. I know now that this place holds no salvation, only torment."

My hands shake as I read on, the words blurring before my eyes. The truth unfolds like a grotesque tapestry, each revelation more horrifying than the last.

"Day 3: The shadows move when no one is looking. I hear them whispering in the darkness, calling to me from beyond the veil of sanity. I try to shut them out, but they seep into my very soul."

Tears well up in my eyes, blurring the words on the page.

Day 4: Tonight, I saw her—the girl from the room next to mine. Her eyes were vacant, her skin ashen. She whispered to me of unspeakable things, of a darkness that even the shadows fear. I know now that we are not alone in this place, something lurks within these walls, watching, waiting.

My hands tremble as I reach the last entry, penned in a frantic scrawl:

"Day 5: They're coming for me. I can hear them outside my door, their footsteps like echoes of death. Dr. Everett's experiments have unleashed something unspeakable, a force beyond comprehension. I don't know if I'll survive the night."

I swallow hard, forcing myself to continue reading. Each page reveals new atrocities, painting a vivid picture of the suffering endured within these walls.

"I won't let your stories be forgotten," I promise, clutching the journal to my chest. "I'll make them pay for what they've done."

As I gather the items to leave, a chill runs down my spine. The hairs on the back of my neck stand on end, and I know I'm no longer alone.

Slowly, I turn, my heart pounding so loudly I fear it might burst from my chest. There, hovering just inches away, is a translucent figure. A woman, her features twisted in agony, her hospital gown torn and stained.

"You're...you're real." I gasp, stumbling backward.

The ghost reaches out a spectral hand, her eyes pleading. I can almost feel the weight of her suffering, pressing down on me like a physical force.

"What do you want?" I ask, my voice barely above a whisper. "How can I help you?"

But before she can respond, the figure fades, dissipating like mist in the morning sun. Her anguished expression is the last thing to vanish, searing itself into my memory.

I stand there, shaking, the room once again silent save for the dripping of water and my own ragged breathing.

"I won't let you down," I promise the empty air. "Any of you. I'll find the truth, regardless of what it costs me."

I clutch the stolen artifacts to my chest and stumble towards the exit, my legs trembling beneath me. The hydrotherapy room seems to close in, its walls pulsing with malevolent energy. I force myself to breathe, to focus on each step.

"One foot in front of the other, Abi," I mutter to myself. "You've survived worse than this."

As I reach the doorway, I pause, my hand hovering over the rusted handle. A part of me wants to turn back, to uncover more secrets hidden in this chamber of horrors. But the rational part of my fractured mind knows I've pushed my luck far enough for one night.

I step into the hallway; the door creaking shut behind me with a finality that sends shivers down my spine. The corridor stretches before me, a yawning abyss of shadows and whispered terrors.

"I did it," I whisper, a hint of pride creeping into my voice. "I faced the darkness and came out alive."

But even as I speak the words, doubt gnaws at the edges of my consciousness. The asylum seems to respond; the air growing thick.

"You think you've won?" a disembodied voice hisses in my ear. "This is only the beginning."

I whirl around, heart pounding, but there's nothing there. Just the endless corridor and the weight of unseen eyes upon me.

"No," I say firmly, clutching the stolen items tighter. "I won't let you break me again. I'm stronger now."

As I make my way back through the decaying halls, my mind races with the implications of what I've discovered. The journals, the photographs, the ghostly encounter—each piece a fragment of a larger, more terrifying puzzle.

"Dr. Everett," I growl, anger burning in my chest. "What kind of monster were you? What did you do to us?"

The asylum creaks and groans around me, as if in response to my questions. I quicken my pace, eager to return to the relative safety of my hidden sanctuary.

"I'm close," I murmur, determination steeling my resolve. "So close to uncovering the truth. But at what cost?"

As I round the last corner, a chill runs down my spine. For a moment, just a fleeting instant, I could swear I saw a figure in a white coat disappearing through a wall. Dr. Everett's ghost? Or just another fracture in my already splintered psyche?

I shake my head, clearing the cobwebs of fear and doubt. "Focus, Abi. One step at a time. You've got what you came for. Now use it."

With a deep breath, I push open the door to my makeshift lair, ready to delve into the horrors I've unearthed. The true challenge, I realize, is only just beginning.

Chapter Twelve

I press my back against the cold, damp wall, my heart thundering in my chest like a caged beast desperate for escape. The asylum corridors stretch before me, a labyrinth of shadows and whispers. Each flickering bulb casts grotesque shapes that dance and twist, mocking my attempts at stealth.

"You can't hide forever," a voice hisses in my ear, though I know it's just another phantom born from the depths of my fractured mind.

I inch forward, my bare feet silent on the grimy floor. Every nerve in my body screams for me to run, but I force myself to move slowly. The weight of unseen eyes presses down on me, and I wonder if the very walls of Crossroads are alive, watching my every move.

As I round a corner, a distant wail echoes through the halls, sending shivers down my spine. Is it a fellow inmate, lost in their own personal hell? Or something far more sinister?

"Keep moving, Abi," I whisper to myself, my voice barely audible. "You're almost there."

The door to my room looms before me, a portal to relative safety in this house of horrors. I reach out with trembling fingers, grasping the cold metal of the handle. As I slowly push it open, the hinges emit a long, agonized creak that seems to reverberate through the entire asylum.

I freeze, my breath caught in my throat. Has anyone heard? Will they come for me now, drag me back to that room where nightmares are born?

"Please," I plead silently to whatever forces might be listening, "let me make it inside."

The gap widens, revealing the familiar confines of my cell-like room. It's hardly a sanctuary, but right now, it's the closest thing to home I have in this twisted world.

As I step across the threshold, a memory flashes unbidden through my mind—the experiments, the pain, the feeling of my very essence being torn apart and reassembled. I stumble, catching myself on the door frame.

"No," I growl, pushing the images away. "Not now. I won't let you control me."

With a last glance down the corridor, I slip inside, knowing that for now, at least, I've evaded detection. But in Crossroads, safety is always an illusion, and tomorrow may bring horrors beyond imagining.

As I take a single step into my room, a looming shadow suddenly materializes in the doorway. My heart leaps into my throat, choking off a scream. Dr. Harker stands before me, his piercing eyes locking onto mine with predatory intensity.

"Going somewhere, Abigale?" His voice is soft, gentle, but laced with an undercurrent of menace that makes my skin crawl.

I stumble backward, my legs threatening to give way beneath me. "I...I was just..." The words die on my tongue as Dr. Harker's imposing figure fills the door frame, blocking any hope of escape.

His cold, calculating gaze rakes over me, dissecting every tremor, every flicker of fear in my eyes. I feel exposed, as if he can peer directly into the chaotic swirl of my thoughts.

"Your nocturnal wanderings are most...intriguing," he muses, a hint of fascination creeping into his clinical tone. "Perhaps we've underestimated the progress of your cognitive enhancement."

The room seems to shrink around us; the air grows stale. Dr. Harker's presence radiates an aura of controlled malevolence that threatens to suffocate me.

I want to scream, to lash out, to do anything but stand here paralyzed by terror. But my body refuses to obey, leaving me trapped in this nightmare made flesh.

"Come now," Dr. Harker says, extending a hand towards me. "It's time for another session. We have so much to explore in that fascinating mind of yours."

My heart pounds a frantic rhythm against my ribs. Another session. More pain. More fragmentation of my already fractured psyche. I can't. I won't.

As Dr. Harker's cold eyes bore into mine, I realize with sickening clarity that I have no choice. In this world, my sanity and soul mean nothing as I'm reduced to a subject, a puzzle to solve.

Panic surges through me like an electric current, jolting my frozen limbs into action. I pivot on my heel, lunging for the shadowy recesses of the room, desperate to put distance between myself and the living embodiment of my nightmares.

"No!" I scream, my voice raw and primal. "Stay away from me!"

But Dr. Harker moves with inhuman speed, his long fingers clamping around my arm like a vice. Where I can feel bruises blooming beneath his grip, a physical manifestation of the terror that threatens to consume me.

"Now, now, Abigale," he chides, his voice a sickening blend of reproach and fascination. "You know better than to resist. It only makes things...more difficult."

I twist and writhe, my body contorting as I struggle against his unyielding hold. The room spins around me, a kaleidoscope of shadows and fractured memories. I see flashes of past torments, of needles and restraints, of pain beyond imagining.

"Let me go!" I snarl, surprising myself with the ferocity in my tone. "I'm not your lab rat, not your...your experiment!"

Dr. Harker's grip tightens, and I can feel the cruel amusement radiating from him. "Oh, but you are so much more than that, my dear. You are the key to unlocking the very essence of human potential."

As I thrash against him, something stirs within me, a power born of desperation and defiance. It pulses beneath my skin, whispering of hidden strengths and untapped abilities.

"You can't...you can't do this," I pant, my voice trembling with a mixture of fear and newfound resolve.

The struggle intensifies, our bodies locked in a grotesque dance of domination and rebellion. My heart pounds like a war drum, each beat echoing through the cavernous room. Dr. Harker's labored breathing mingles with my own, creating a discordant symphony of desperation.

"Your resistance is...fascinating," he grunts, his clinical detachment wavering for a moment. "But ultimately futile."

I feel my strength waning, my limbs growing heavier with each passing second. The scuffling of our feet against the cold floor creates a rhythmic scraping that seems to count down my remaining moments of freedom.

"No!" I scream, my voice raw and primal. "I won't go back there!"

But Dr. Harker's determination is unwavering. His face, usually a mask of cold calculation, now bears an unsettling blankness as he drags me towards the torture room. I know that look—it's the absence of empathy, the void where compassion should reside.

"The work must continue, Abigale," he states flatly, as if discussing the weather. "Your mind holds secrets. We've only begun to unravel."

As we near the dreaded door, panic claws at my insides. My thoughts race, fragmented and chaotic. What fresh horrors await me beyond that threshold? What pieces of myself will I lose this time?

"Please," I whimper, a final, desperate plea. "There has to be another way."

Dr. Harker's grip remains unrelenting, his resolve as unyielding as the asylum's stone walls. My bare feet drag against the icy floor, each step a torturous scrape that sends shivers up my spine. As the door looms before us, the last vestiges of hope slipping away, replaced by a terrifying certainty that whatever lies ahead will reshape me in ways I cannot fathom.

"Let me go!" I shriek, my voice echoing through the empty corridors. "Someone, anyone, help me!"

Dr. Harker's breath is hot against my ear as he hisses, "Your cries are futile, Abigale. No one can hear you. No one will come."

My mind reels, fragments of memories and fears colliding. I see flashes of past torments, of needles and restraints, of Dr. Harker's cold eyes watching as I writhe in agony.

"You can't do this," I pant, still struggling. "I'm not just your experiment. I'm a person!"

He chuckles darkly. "Oh, Abigale. You're so much more than a person. You're the key to unlocking the mind's true potential."

I feel my strength ebbing, my resistance weakening with each step towards that dreaded room. The asylum's silence is deafening, swallowing my pleas whole. In this moment, I realize the true horror of Crossroads—not just the pain inflicted within its walls, but the absolute isolation it represents.

"Please," I whimper one last time, my voice barely a whisper. "I don't want to lose myself again."

The only response is the echo of our footsteps and the creaking of that final, terrible door as it opens to swallow me whole.

My eyes dart frantically, searching for an escape that doesn't exist. The flickering lights cast grotesque shadows on the walls, morphing into nightmarish shapes that mock my desperation. Each step closer to the torture room feels like a death knell, my legs growing heavier, as if weighed down by invisible chains.

"You don't understand," I plead, my voice cracking. "There are things in my head...things you've put there. They're tearing me apart!"

Dr. Harker's grip tightens, his fingers digging into my flesh. "That's precisely why we must continue, Abigale. Your mind is on the brink of a breakthrough."

The last vestiges of hope slip away, replaced by a cold, creeping dread. "A breakthrough? Or a breakdown?" I whisper, more to myself than to him.

The doctor doesn't respond, his silence more terrifying than any words could be. We reach the door, its metal surface scarred and pitted, a testament to the horrors it has witnessed.

"No, no, no," I mutter, my mantra of denial growing more frantic.

With a swift motion, Dr. Harker pushes me forward. I stumble, my hands outstretched to break my fall. The room looms before me, a yawning abyss of pain and fear.

"Welcome back, Abigale," Dr. Harker intones, his voice devoid of emotion. "Let's see what secrets your mind will reveal today."

The door slams shut with a finality that echoes through my very soul. I'm alone with my tormentor, surrounded by instruments of suffering both familiar and unknown. As the lock clicks into place, something inside me shatters, and I wonder if this time, I'll lose myself for good.

Chapter Thirteen

Chapter Thirteen

I jolt awake, my heart a frenzied drumbeat against my ribs. The darkness presses in, suffocating, as if the very air seeks to crush me. My eyes dart wildly, searching for...what? A threat? A savior? In this place, they're often the same.

"Not again," I whisper, my voice a ragged thing barely escaping my throat. "Please, not again."

But the unease coiling in my gut tells me it's already too late. The asylum has me in its grasp, and it won't let go easily.

A flicker catches my eye, a dance of light and shadow in the far corner.

I should look away. I should curl up, squeeze my eyes shut, and pray for morning. But that damned curiosity, the one that's always gotten me into trouble, tugs at me.

"What are you?" I murmur, swinging my legs over the edge of the threadbare mattress. The floor creaks ominously as I stand, and I imagine it might give way, plunging me into some nightmare realm below.

But I take a step. Then another.

"Are you here to hurt me?" I ask, the flickering light inching closer. "Or are you showing me something?"

My heart pounds harder with each step. The shadows twist and writhe, forming shapes that vanish before I can truly make them out. Are those faces in the darkness? Hands reaching out?

I squeeze my eyes shut for a moment, willing the visions away. "It's not real," I tell myself, but I don't even believe it anymore. Here, in Crossroads, the line between reality and madness is as thin as spider silk.

Opening my eyes, I find myself mere inches from the source of the light. It dances just beyond my fingertips, hypnotic and terrifying. Dare I reach out and touch it?

"What secrets are you hiding?" I whisper, my voice trembling. "What horrors are you about to unleash?"

As if in answer, the light pulses brighter, casting my shadow huge and distorted against the far wall. For a moment, it doesn't look human at all.

The light coalesces, forming a spectral figure that hovers before me. Its edges ripple and blur, like smoke caught in a breeze. My breath catches in my throat as I realize this is no mere malfunction—it's an apparition, ethereal and haunting.

"Who...who are you?" I stammer, my voice barely above a whisper. The chill that runs down my spine is visceral, as if icy fingers are tracing my vertebrae one by one.

The ghostly form remains silent, its featureless face turned towards me. I can feel its gaze, heavy and probing, as if it's peering into the darkest corners of my fractured mind.

"Please," I plead, taking a hesitant step forward. "I need to know. Are you here to help me or...or to harm me?"

Silence stretches between us, broken only by the pounding of my heart. The walls of my room seem to close in, threatening to drown me in the misery they hold.

"Speak to me!" I cry out, desperation clawing at my insides. "What do you want from me?"

The apparition's form wavers, growing brighter for a moment before dimming again. Is it communicating? Or is this another cruel trick of my fragmented psyche?

I reach out, my fingers trembling as they pass through the ghostly light. A jolt of electricity courses through me, and for a split second, I see flashes of memories or are they premonitions that aren't my own. Screams echo in my mind, I smell the acrid stench of fear and despair.

Gasping, I stumble backward, my legs hitting the edge of the bed. "What are you showing me?" I whisper, my voice breaking. "What horrors await in the depths of this asylum?"

The apparition remains maddeningly silent, its presence a cold weight in the room. I feel caught between terror and an insatiable need to understand, to unravel the mysteries that have plagued me since I first arrived at Crossroads.

"I won't let you break me," I say, forcing steel into my voice even as fear threatens to overwhelm me. "Whatever you are, whatever you want, I'll face it. I must."

Suddenly, a violent gust of wind tears through the room, rattling the windowpanes and sending a chill down my spine. The ghostly light flickers wildly, its ethereal form twisting and contorting before it's snuffed out completely. Darkness engulfs me.

"No!" I gasp, my heart pounding against my rib cage. My eyes flick frantically, adjusting to the pitch-black surroundings. "Come back!"

I stumble forward, arms outstretched, grasping at empty air. My foot catches on something—a loose floorboard?—and I nearly fall. The darkness feels alive, pressing in on me from all sides.

"Where are you?" I whisper, my voice trembling. "I need answers!"

As if in response, a chorus of whispers erupts around me. They come from everywhere and nowhere, hisses that make my skin crawl.

"Who's there?" I demand, spinning in place. My heightened senses strain against the darkness, picking up fragments of words that chill me to my core.

"...blood...sacrifice...chosen..."

"What does that mean?" I cry out, pressing my hands against my ears. The whispers penetrate my defenses, slithering into my mind like poisonous tendrils.

"...darkness...rises... Abigale..."

My name on their lips sends a jolt of terror through me. "How do you know me?" I ask, my voice barely audible over the rising tide of whispers.

The voices grow louder, more insistent, swirling around me in a dizzying vortex. I spin, tracking their source, but they seem to come from every direction at once. My breath comes in sharp gasps as panic claws at my throat.

"Stop it!" I scream, dropping to my knees and clutching my head. "Leave me alone!"

But the whispers persist, their words becoming a twisted mantra that echoes through the suffocating darkness of my room—my prison—in Crossroads Asylum.

As I crawl on my hands and knees, desperate to escape the maddening whispers, my fingers brush against something different. A faint warmth emanates from the wall, and I pause, heart racing. Squinting through the darkness, I notice a soft glow seeping through a hairline crack in the wallpaper.

"What?" I murmur, tracing the outline with trembling fingers. The whispers fade to a dull roar as I focus on this new discovery.

Curiosity wars with fear as I peel back the wallpaper, revealing a hidden door and passage. A pale, sickly light spills out, barely illuminating the cramped opening. I hesitate, torn between the unknown dangers that, I think, will lurk within and the relentless terror of the darkness behind me.

"Is this real?" I wonder aloud, my voice small and uncertain. "Or just another trick of my fractured mind?"

The whispers surge again, as if sensing my indecision. Their snake-like hisses urge me forward, driving me towards the passage with a primal fear I can't shake.

"Okay," I breathe, steeling myself. "Nowhere to go but forward."

With shaking hands, I pull myself into the narrow corridor. The walls press in close, slick with moisture and cold as death. Each step sends shivers down my spine, the damp chill seeping into my bones.

"Keep it together, Abi," I mutter.

As I venture deeper, it's as if the very walls are alive, pulsing with dark secrets and forgotten horrors. My breath comes in quick gasps, echoing in the confined space.

"What is this place?" I whisper, more to hear a human voice than expect an answer. "What other nightmares are you hiding, Crossroads?"

The pale light flickers, casting grotesque shadows that seem to reach for me with grasping fingers. I press on, driven by a desperate need to escape, even as every instinct screams at me to turn back.

The passage twists unexpectedly, and I stumble, my shoulder slamming against the damp wall. "Damn it," I hiss, the pain momentarily cutting through my fear. As I right myself, I realize I've lost all sense of direction. Which way leads back to my room? Which way leads...where?

Chapter Fourteen

"Hello?" I call out, my voice trembling. "Is anyone there?"

The silence that follows is deafening, broken only by the rapid pounding of my heart. Then, a sound pierces the quiet—a distant scream, raw and agonized, echoing through the hidden corridor.

I freeze, every muscle in my body tensing. "That's not real," I tell myself, even as my skin prickles with goosebumps. "It's just another hallucination. It has to be."

But then I hear it: footsteps. Slow, deliberate, coming from somewhere behind me. The scraping of metal against stone follows, a grating sound that sets my teeth on edge.

"Who's there?" I demand, my voice cracking with fear. I spin around, peering into the darkness behind me. "Show yourself!"

The footsteps stop abruptly, leaving only the echo of that terrible scraping. My breath comes in short, panicked gasps as I press myself against the wall, hoping to make myself as small as possible.

"This isn't happening," I whisper, squeezing my eyes shut. "It's all in your head, Abi. Just like before. Just like always."

But when I open my eyes, the passage seems to have narrowed even further; the walls pressing in on me with suffocating intensity. I can't tell if it's real or just my paranoia twisting my perception.

"I have to keep moving," I mutter, forcing myself to take one step, then another. "I can't stay here. I can't let them find me."

As I push forward, the unsettling sounds continue to reverberate through the passage, a symphony of horrors that threatens to unravel what's left of my sanity.

WELCOME TO THE ASYLUM

A searing pain lances through my skull, and suddenly, I'm no longer in the passage. Flashes of horrific images bombard my mind, each more vivid and disturbing than the last. I see bodies strapped to gurneys, their mouths open in silent screams. Shadowy figures in lab coats loom over them, wielding scalpels that glint ominously in the dim light.

"No, no, no," I whimper, clutching my head. "Not again. Please, not again."

The visions shift, and I'm looking through the eyes of a young girl—myself, years ago. I'm huddled in a corner, watching as orderlies drag a thrashing patient down the hall. His screams echo in my ears, mingling with my own terrified sobs.

"It's not real," I gasp, stumbling forward. "It's just memories. Just the past."

The line between past and present blurs as another vision overtakes me. I see myself strapped to a chair, electrodes attached to my temples. A doctor looms over me, his face obscured by shadows.

"This is for your own good, Abigale," he says, his voice dripping with false kindness. "We're going to make you all better."

I scream as phantom electricity courses through my body, leaving me trembling and weak. When I open my eyes, I find myself on my knees in a dilapidated hallway. I've emerged from the hidden passage into a forgotten wing of the asylum.

"Where am I?" I whisper, looking around at the deteriorating walls. The air feels as if the very building is trying to crush me beneath its weight of dark secrets.

I struggle to my feet, my legs shaking beneath me. "Hello?" I call out, my voice echoing in the empty corridor. "Is anyone there?"

Only silence answers me, but I can't shake the feeling that I'm being watched. The walls seem to pulse with violent energy, and I swear I can hear whispers just beyond the edge of hearing.

"I have to get out of here," I mutter, wrapping my arms around myself. "I can't let them find me. I can't go back."

As I take a hesitant step forward, the floorboards creak ominously beneath my feet. I freeze, my heart pounding in my chest as I wait for something to happen. But the silence persists, broken only by my ragged breathing.

"You're stronger than this, Abi," I tell myself, forcing to keep moving.

I make my way down the corridor, with the feeling that I'm walking deeper into the belly of the beast. And somewhere in the depths of this forgotten wing, something is waiting for me.

A flicker of movement catches my eye, and I spin around, my breath catching in my throat. There, in the shadows at the end of the hallway, I swear I saw a figure dart across my vision.

"Who's there?" I call out, my voice trembling. "Show yourself!"

But the shadowy presence vanishes as quickly as it appeared, leaving me questioning my sanity. Am I seeing things, or are the asylum's dark spirits coming to life around me?

I turn back, only to see another shadow flit past an open doorway to my right. My heart races, adrenaline surging through my veins. "This isn't real," I whisper to myself. "It's just like before. Just another trick of the mind."

But deep down, I know it's not. The air grows colder, and I can feel unseen eyes boring into me from every direction.

"I need to get out," I mutter, breaking into a run. My footsteps echo loudly in the empty corridor, betraying my presence of whatever lurks in the darkness.

I race down the hallway, taking random turns, desperate to find an exit. But each corner I round only leads to another identical corridor, the asylum's layout a maddening maze designed to trap its inhabitants.

"No, no, no," I pant, reaching another dead end. I spin around, only to see more shadowy figures at the far end of the hallway, their forms indistinct but undeniably menacing.

"Stay away from me!" I scream, backing up against the wall. "I won't let you take me again!"

The shadows seem to pause, as if considering my words. Then, slowly, they advance.

I close my eyes, willing myself to wake up from this nightmare. But when I open them again, the shadows are still there, drawing ever closer.

"Please, someone help me. Anyone..." I whimper, sliding down the wall as despair overwhelms me.

In the depths of Crossroads Asylum, I know my pleas are ignored. The only ones who can hear me now are the spirits of the damned, and they offer no comfort, only the promise of eternal torment.

I stumble forward, my heart pounding like a frantic drum in my chest. The corridor stretches before me, an endless maw of darkness threatening to swallow me whole. My fingers trace the disintegrating walls, searching for an escape that seems increasingly elusive.

"There has to be a way out," I mutter, my voice a hoarse whisper in the crushing silence. "Think, Abi, think!"

A flicker of movement catches my eye, and I freeze. Is it another shadow person, or just my frayed nerves playing tricks?

I force myself to keep moving, each step feeling like I'm wading through molasses. The air grows thick, cloying, as if the very atmosphere of Crossroads is trying to kill me.

Then, at the end of the corridor, I see it—a door. Hope flares in my chest, bright and painful.

"Please," I breathe, stumbling towards it. "Please be unlocked."

My trembling hands grasp the rusted handle, and I twist with all my might. It doesn't budge.

"No!" I cry out, pounding my fists against the unyielding metal. "Open! Someone, anyone, please hear me!"

My voice echoes through the empty halls, a desperate plea lost in the asylum's vastness. Tears stream down my face as I continue to beat against the door, each impact sending jolts of pain through my hands.

"I can't stay here," I sob, pressing my forehead against the cold surface. "I can't go back to the experiments, to the pain. Please..."

But only silence answers, broken by the soft whisper of unseen things moving in the shadows behind me.

Chapter Fifteen

The shadows in Dr. Everett's office seem to writhe and dance, mocking me as I stand before his imposing mahogany desk. My heart pounds in my chest, each beat a reminder of the countless horrors I've endured within these accursed walls. I clench my trembling hands into fists, willing my voice not to betray the terror that courses through my veins.

"You...you've been experimenting on me," I accuse, the words tumbling out in a rush. "The nightmares, the lost time, the pain—it's all because of you and your twisted experiments!"

Dr. Everett's cold, gray eyes bore into mine, his face an impassive mask. The corner of his mouth twitches imperceptibly, and I wonder if it's the ghost of a smile or a grimace of annoyance.

"Miss Sheetz," he says, his voice dripping with condescension, "I assure you that your accusations are entirely unfounded. These delusions are merely a manifestation of your troubled psyche."

My mind reels, fragments of memories flashing before my eyes—needles piercing my skin, blinding lights, the acrid smell of chemicals. I struggle to piece them together, to make sense of the horrors that haunt my dreams.

"No," I insist, my voice quavering. "I remember... I remember the tests, the pain. You can't deny it!"

Dr. Everett leans back in his leather chair, steepling his fingers beneath his chin. "Your imagination is vivid, Abigale. We should increase your medication to help quell these...fantasies."

A chill runs down my spine at his words, and I fight the urge to flee. I can't let him dismiss me so easily, can't let him continue his cruel experiments unchallenged.

"They're not fantasies," I say, my voice stronger now, fueled by a desperate need to be heard. "I know what you've done, what you're still doing. You can't hide behind your title forever, Dr. Everett."

He sighs, a sound of exaggerated patience. "Miss Sheetz, I understand that you're distressed, these accusations are not only false, but damaging to your treatment progress."

I feel my resolve wavering under his unwavering gaze, doubt creeping in like tendrils of fog. Am I truly delusional? Are the horrors in my mind nothing more than the product of a broken psyche?

No. I can't let him plant seeds of doubt. I won't let him twist my reality any further.

"You're lying," I whisper, my voice barely audible. "You're lying, and one day, everyone will know the truth about what happens in this asylum."

Dr. Everett's expression hardens, a flash of something dangerous in his eyes. "We're done here, Miss Sheetz. Nurse!" he calls, his voice echoing in the office.

"You can't dismiss me," I snarl, my voice raw with emotion. "The experiments, the pain—it's all real. I remember everything."

"They're not fantasies!" I slam my fist on his desk, papers scattering. "You stripped away my humanity, treated me like a lab rat. I still hear the others crying at night."

Dr. Everett's lips curl into a cold smirk. "Abigale, as I have already stated, your mind is playing tricks on you again. These fantasies—"

His eyes narrow, a predatory gleam replacing his feigned concern. "You've become a nuisance, Miss Sheetz. Perhaps it is time for a more...intensive treatment."

Fear coils in my gut as he reaches for the intercom. "Orderlies to my office. Immediately."

"No," I whisper, backing away. "No, you can't do this."

"I can, and I will," Dr. Everett says, rising from his chair. "You see, Abigale, in here, I am God. And you? You're nothing but a broken mind in need of fixing."

The door bursts open, and two burly orderlies enter. I run, but their hands are on me instantly, rough, and unforgiving.

"Strap her down," Dr. Everett commands, his voice dripping with sadistic glee. "It seems our dear Abigale needs a reminder of her place at this institution."

As they force me onto a nearby gurney, tightening leather straps around my wrists and ankles, I realize with horrifying clarity that my worst nightmares are about to begin anew.

My heart thunders against my rib cage, a frantic drumbeat of terror. I scan the room wildly, desperate for any avenue of escape, finding only sterile walls and clinical instruments that mock my helplessness. The orderlies loom over me, their faces impassive masks as they secure the final strap across my chest.

"Please," I croak, my voice barely above a whisper. "Don't do this."

Dr. Everett's bitter laugh slithers through the air. "Oh, Abigale. Still clinging to hope? How...quaint." He steps closer, his breath hot on my face. "You know, your resilience is truly remarkable. It's what makes you such a perfect subject."

I strain against the restraints, feeling them bite into my skin. "I'm not your subject! I'm a person, damn you!"

"Shh," he soothes, running a finger along my cheek. I flinch away, repulsed. "Soon, you won't have to worry about such trivialities."

He turns to the orderlies, his voice crisp with authority. "Prepare her for total sensory deprivation. Maximum intensity."

As one of them approaches with a black blindfold, panic explodes in my chest. "No! You can't—"

The fabric slides over my eyes, plunging me into darkness. I hear the orderly's grunt as he tightens it, ensuring not a sliver of light penetrates.

"Dr. Everett," I plead, my words muffled by rising hysteria, "whatever I did to offend you, I'm sorry. Please, just talk to me!"

"Now, now," his voice floats from somewhere to my left. "Talking defeats the purpose, doesn't it? You need to learn to exist in silence."

Something heavy settles over my ears—noise-canceling headphones. The last thing I hear before they're switched on is Dr. Everett's parting words:

"Welcome to oblivion, Abigale."

Nothing. An all-consuming void swallows me whole, leaving me adrift in a sea of nothingness. I scream, but even that is stolen from me, lost in the deafening silence of my mind.

WELCOME TO THE ASYLUM

The void consumes me, a hungry beast devouring every shred of reality. I thrash against the restraints, my muscles screaming as I struggle. The darkness is pressing against my skin like a living thing. I can't breathe. I can't think.

"Let me out!" I scream, but the words die in my throat, swallowed by the silence. My mind races, fragments of memories and nightmares colliding in a kaleidoscope of terror. I see flashes of my past—the troubled teenager I once was, the curiosity that led me down this path of torment.

I strain my ears, desperate for any sound, any connection to the world beyond this prison of sensory deprivation. But there's nothing. Just the thunderous beating of my heart echoing in the vast emptiness of my skull.

"Please," I whisper, my lips moving soundlessly. "I'm still here. I'm still me."

But am I? With each passing moment, pieces of myself slipping away, dissolving into the darkness. Who am I without sight, without sound? What remains when everything is stripped away?

I imagine Dr. Everett watching me, his cold eyes gleaming with satisfaction. In my mind's eye, I see his thin lips curled into a smile, reveling in my torment. He thinks he's breaking me, molding me into something new. But he doesn't understand. This void, this nothingness—it's forging me into something stronger, something he can't control.

"You won't win," I mouth the words, a silent defiance in the face of his cruelty. "I'll find a way out. I always do."

My body convulses, a primal scream tearing from my throat. The sound is muffled, swallowed by the stifling silence, but it vibrates through my chest. It's a raw, animalistic cry that echoes the chaos swirling in my mind.

"Let me out!" I shriek, thrashing against the restraints. The leather bites into my skin, but the pain is welcome–a reminder that I still exist. "Please, I can't... I can't..."

My words dissolve into incoherent sobs. Tears soak the blindfold, the dampness a stark contrast to the dryness of my mouth. I'm unanchored in a sea of unyielding pitch; the shoreline of sanity is rapidly receding.

"Fascinating," I imagine Dr. Everett murmuring, his pen scratching across his notepad. "Subject exhibits extreme distress under prolonged sensory deprivation."

Rage flares within me, hot and bright against the void. "I'm not your subject! Even though I know he can't hear me, I wail. I'm human!"

But am I? The boundaries of myself are blurring, melting away like wax under a flame. I see faces in the darkness—my younger self, wide-eyed and curious; Dr. Harker, his piercing gaze promising answers I never wanted; and others, shadowy figures from the depths of Crossroads Asylum.

"Stay with me," I whisper to myself, clinging to the fragments of my identity.

But have I? The silence stretches on, an eternity compressed into each agonizing second. Despite that, beyond my private hell, I know Dr. Everett watches, waits, and records every moment of my descent into madness.

Suddenly, light sears my retinas as the blindfold is ripped away. The cacophony of the world rushes back, overwhelming my senses. I blink rapidly, focusing on Dr. Everett's face looming above me.

"Experiment concluded," he announces, his voice devoid of emotion. "Release the patient."

As the orderlies unbuckle my restraints, I struggle to piece together coherent thoughts. "Why?" I croak, my throat raw from screaming. "What did you hope to achieve?"

Dr. Everett regards me with cold detachment. "Progress, Miss Sheetz. The mind's resilience under extreme stress is...illuminating."

I sit up shakily, rubbing my wrists. The room spins, and I fight the urge to vomit. "You call this progress? You're a monster."

He smiles thinly. "Monsters often pave the way for breakthroughs, my dear. Your contribution to science is...appreciated."

As he turns to leave, a fragment of memory surfaces—Dr. Harker's voice, whispering: "The mind holds secrets we've only begun to unlock."

I clutch my head, holding on to the thought. "Wait," I call out. "Dr. Harker...he knew something. About my mind. What was it?"

Dr. Everett pauses at the door, his expression unreadable. "Dr. Harker's theories were...unorthodox. Rest now, Abigale. We have much work ahead of us."

The door clicks shut behind him, leaving me alone with the scattered pieces of my spirit. I curl into myself, shivering, as the asylum's smothering silence settles around me once more.

Chapter Sixteen

The shadows writhe on the walls like tormented souls, their dance a macabre reminder of where I am. I jolt awake, heart pounding, sheets damp with cold sweat. Another night of fragmented nightmares, of screams that, I think, will be my own.

"Not real," I whisper, the words ring hollow in the silence of my room at the hospital.

As I sit up, a chill creeps along my spine. Something's different. A presence, an energy, pulling at the frayed edges of my subconscious. I swing my legs over the bed, bare feet touching the icy floor.

"Who's there?" I ask the darkness. No answer comes, yet the feeling intensifies.

I stand, drawn by an inexplicable urge. My fingers trail along the flaking walls as I move to the door. It creaks open, revealing the yawning maw of the corridor beyond.

"I shouldn't," I murmur, but my body has other ideas. I step into the hallway, guided by an unseen force.

The asylum passages stretch before me, a maze of decay and forgotten pain. I wander, lost in the twisting corridors, until I come upon a door I've never noticed before. Its rusted hinges groan in protest as I push it open.

A storage room, long abandoned. Dust motes dance in the pale moonlight filtering through a grimy window. My eyes are drawn to a box in the corner, its contents spilling onto the floor.

I kneel, fingers trembling as I lift a yellowed photograph. A face stares back at me, eyes hollow with despair. Another photo, another lost soul. Another and another.

"What happened to you?" I whisper, my voice thick with emotion. "What secrets are you telling me?"

The photographs seem to pulse with latent energy, each one a window into the asylum's dark past. I rifle through them, my breath catching as recognition dawns.

"I've seen you before," I gasp, memories flooding back of faces glimpsed in nightmares and visions. "You're showing me something, aren't you?"

A gust of wind rustles the papers, sending a chill through my thin nightgown. I clutch the box to my chest, knowing what I've stumbled upon is something important, something dangerous.

"I'll find out what happened here," I promise the ghosts of Crossroads. "I'll make it right."

As I turn to leave, the shadows seem to coalesce, watching me with hungry anticipation. My mind is racing with possibilities and fears. Whatever secrets this asylum holds, I'm now bound to uncover them, no matter the cost to my already fractured sanity.

My hands shake as I sift through the dusty records, each page revealing new horrors. My heart sinks deeper with every revelation, an icy dread seeping into my bones.

"No...it can't be," I whisper, Dr. Harker's name appearing repeatedly, always connected to the most horrific cases. "What have you done?"

I trace his signature on a gruesome report, my fingertips tingling with an otherworldly energy. Suddenly, the world around me blurs, and I'm no longer in the storage room.

Icy water laps at my skin, and I gasp, finding myself in a rusted tub. The hydrotherapy room materializes around me, its walls echoing with screams of agony.

"Please, no more!" a voice cries out, and I whirl to see a gaunt figure thrashing in another tub.

"It's not real," I remind myself, squeezing my eyes shut. "It's just a vision."

But the terror feels all too real, the memories of countless patients flooding my mind. I see Dr. Harker looming over them, his eyes cold and calculating as he observes their suffering.

"Fascinating," his voice echoes in my head. "Push them further. We must break their minds to rebuild them."

I clutch my temples, overwhelmed by the barrage of images. "Stop," I plead, but the visions keep coming, each more horrifying than the last.

When I open my eyes, I'm back in the storage room, gasping for air. The records are scattered around me, silent witnesses to the asylum's dark past.

"Dr. Harker," I breathe, a mix of fear and determination coursing through me. "What kind of monster are you?"

The world spins, and I collapse to the cold, unforgiving floor. My lungs burn, desperate for air that seems to have fled the room. I clutch my head, fingernails digging into my scalp as if I could physically tear the horrific images from my mind.

"Make it stop," I whimper, my voice a broken whisper in the silence.

The visions won't relent. Assaulting my senses, a cacophony of tortured wails and the acrid smell of fear. I see faces contorted in agony, bodies writhing in restraints, and always, always, Dr. Harker's cold eyes observing it all.

"Why?" I cry out, my body curling into itself. "Why did you do this to us?"

As suddenly as they began, the visions recede, leaving me trembling on the floor. I gulp in the air, my chest heaving. Slowly, painfully, I push myself up, my arms shaking with the effort.

"I can't let this continue," I mutter, wiping sweat from my brow. "I have to stop him."

A strange calm settles over me, born of desperation and newfound purpose. I stand, my legs unsteady but my resolve unshakeable.

"Dr. Harker," I say to the empty room, my voice growing stronger with each word, "your reckoning has come."

I take a step toward the door, then another. My footsteps echo in the corridor, a grim metronome counting down to confrontation.

"I'm coming for you," I whisper, my words carried on the asylum's stale air. "And I'll make you face every horror you've inflicted."

The door to Dr. Harker's office looms before me, a monolith of dark, polished wood. My hand trembles as I reach for the tarnished brass knob, its cold surface biting into my palm. I turn it slowly, the mechanism's soft click echoing in the stillness.

As I push the door open, the hinges groan in protest, as if warning me to turn back. The room beyond is a sepulcher of knowledge and madness. Towering bookshelves line the walls, their contents a mix of respected medical tomes and esoteric volumes with titles that make my skin crawl. The air is thick with the scent of old paper and something metallic—something that reminds me of blood.

In the center of this literary complex, hunched over a cluttered desk, sits Dr. Harker. His unkempt hair falls across his forehead as he scribbles furiously in a leather-bound journal. He doesn't look up as I enter, too engrossed in whatever twisted musings flow from his pen.

"Dr. Harker," I say, my voice quavering despite my efforts to steady it.

He pauses, his pen hovering above the page. Slowly, he raises his head, and those piercing eyes lock onto mine. A chill runs down my spine.

"Abigale," he says, his tone maddeningly calm. "To what do I owe this...interruption?"

I clench my fists, anger surging through me. "You know why I'm here," I spit out. "The experiments, the torture—I've seen it all. How could you do this to us?"

Dr. Harker's face remains impassive, a mask of clinical detachment. "Experiments?" he echoes, raising an eyebrow. "I prefer to think of them as necessary steps toward enlightenment."

His words fuel the fire burning within me. I want to scream, to lash out, to make him feel a fraction of the pain he's caused. But beneath my rage, fear lingers. What if he's right? What if I'm just another broken mind, imagining horrors?

No. I can't doubt myself now. The memories are too vivid, too real.

"Enlightenment?" I echo, my voice dripping with bitter sarcasm. "Is that what you call drowning patients in ice baths? Shocking them until they can't remember their own names?"

Dr. Harker stands, his movement fluid and predatory. He towers over me, his presence filling the room. "My dear," he says, his voice soft but laced with danger, "you cannot comprehend the importance of my work."

I stand my ground, even as every instinct screams at me to run. "Try me," I challenge, meeting his gaze.

Chapter Seventeen

Dr. Harker's lips curl into a cruel smile. "Your so-called psychic abilities," he sneers, "nothing more than the delusions of a fractured mind. Tell me, Abigale, how can you trust your perceptions when your reality is so...unstable?"

His words cut deep, probing at my deepest insecurities. For a moment, the world seems to tilt around me, doubt creeping in like a poisonous fog. But then it—a spark of defiance igniting within my core.

"No," I whisper, then louder, "No! You don't get to twist this."

I close my eyes, reaching deep into the well of power I've always feared. The air around us crackles with unseen energy. When I open my eyes, the room has fallen away, replaced by a swirling vortex of memories and emotions.

Dr. Harker's eyes widen in shock as I plunge into his mind. Images flash before us—patients strapped to chairs, screaming as electricity courses through their bodies; dark figures huddled over operating tables, scalpels glinting in harsh light; a young girl sobbing in a padded cell, her pleas ignored.

"This is the truth," I say, my voice echoing strangely in this mental landscape. "Your cruelty, your obsession, laid bare."

Dr. Harker struggles against my psychic grip, his carefully constructed walls crumbling. I push deeper, exposing the rot at his core—the insatiable hunger for knowledge, the belief that any price is worth paying for progress.

"Stop this!" he snarls, but I'm beyond his control now.

I am the judge, the jury, and the executioner of his darkest secrets.

Dr. Harker's face contorts, a mask of fury and terror. "You insolent wretch!" he screams, spittle flying from his lips. "You do not know what you're meddling with!"

His composure shatters like brittle glass, revealing the monster beneath. I watch as he claws at his desk, scattering papers and upending a jar of pens. The crash echoes through the dim office, but I stand my ground, a strange calm settling over me.

"I know exactly what I'm dealing with, doctor," I say, my voice steady despite the trembling in my limbs. "A man so consumed by his quest for power that he's lost all humanity."

Dr. Harker lunges towards me, his eyes wild. "You're nothing but a lab rat!" he shrieks. "A broken mind I sought to fix!"

I sidestep his attack, my newfound strength surprising us both. In this moment, I see him for what he truly is—a scared, desperate man clinging to control.

"Fix?" I laugh, the sound harsh and unfamiliar. "You never wanted to heal us. You wanted to own us, to reshape our minds into weapons for your ambition."

As I speak, the asylum itself is listening, the walls seeming to lean in. The air grows thick with the weight of countless souls who've suffered within these walls.

Dr. Harker stumbles back, his facade crumbling further. "You don't understand," he pleads, a note of desperation creeping into his voice. "The potential...the breakthroughs we could achieve..."

I shake my head, feeling a surge of pity beneath my anger. "No, doctor. The only thing you've achieved is creating a monument to your ego."

With a final push of my abilities, I lay bare the truth of his motivations. The room fills with ghostly images—Dr. Harker receiving accolades, his name in scientific journals, the adoration of the masses. Beneath it all, a gnawing emptiness, an insatiable need to prove his brilliance at any cost.

"This is what drives you," I mumble. "Not the advancement of science, but your own glory."

Dr. Harker crumples to the floor, a broken man faced with the stark reality of his actions. And I, Abigale Sheetz, stand tall for the first time in years, ready to reclaim my life and fight for those who can't.

I turn away from Dr. Harker's crumpled form, my heart pounding so hard I can feel it in my throat. The victory feels hollow, tainted by the weight of all the suffering that led to this moment. As I grasp the cold doorknob, I pause, stealing one last glance at the broken man behind me.

"This isn't over," I whisper, more to myself than to him. "There's still so much to uncover, so many wrongs to right."

The corridor stretches before me, dimly lit and cold. My footsteps echo off the shedding walls as I make my way through the dank hallways of Crossroads. Each step feels like a minor act of defiance against the horrors that have transpired here.

Suddenly, a chill runs down my spine. The surrounding air seems to thicken, charged with an otherworldly energy. Whispers, barely audible, brush against my consciousness.

"Do you feel them?" I murmur, my eyes darting from shadow to shadow. "The ones who came before...they're here with us."

As if in response, a gust of wind rushes past me, carrying with it the faint scent of antiseptic and despair. The flickering lights above cast dancing shadows that seem to reach out toward me.

"I hear you," I say, my voice trembling. "I know what happened here. And I promise, I won't let your stories be forgotten."

The whispers grow more insistent, a cacophony of pleas and warnings that threaten to overwhelm me. I press my palms against my temples, making sense of the fragmented messages.

"Show me," I implore, opening my mind to the spirits that linger here. "Show me what I need to see."

In that moment, the corridor dissolves around me, replaced by fleeting visions of patients strapped to beds, of cruel experiments conducted in the name of progress. The weight of their collective suffering is unbearable, but I force myself to bear witness.

As the visions fade, I find myself back in the corridor, gasping for breath. But now, a renewed sense of purpose coursing through my veins.

"I understand now," I say, straightening my shoulders. "This place...it's more than just an asylum. It's a testament to human cruelty, and a warning of what can happen when we lose sight of humanity."

With each step forward, the presence of those lost souls walking beside me, urging me onward. Their whispers have become a rallying cry, spurring me towards the truth that lies hidden within these walls.

"We're not finished yet," I declare to the empty corridor, my voice growing stronger. "There are still secrets to uncover, and I won't rest until every last one is brought into the light."

I press my trembling hand against the damp wallpaper, feeling the asylum's dark history pulsing beneath my fingertips. The flickering lights cast dancing shadows, and for a moment, I swear I see faces in their depths—the forgotten patients, their eyes pleading for justice.

"I need allies," I whisper, my voice barely audible over the constant creaking of the building. "I can't do this alone."

As if in response, a faint cry echoes from down the hall. I follow the sound, my bare feet silent on the cold floor. I find myself outside the common room, where a handful of patients spend their days in a drug-induced haze.

Not only that, I push open the heavy door, wincing at its rusty groan. Inside, a few familiar faces turn towards me, their eyes clouded with confusion and fear.

"Listen to me," I say, my voice cracking with urgency. "We've all suffered here, but we're not powerless. Dr. Harker—he's been experimenting on us, torturing us. I've seen the truth, and we can expose him."

A gaunt man named Thomas shakes his head. "You're crazy, Abi. Crazier than the rest of us."

I laugh, a bitter sound that surprises even me. "I am. But that doesn't mean I'm wrong. Haven't you felt it? The wrongness in this place?"

Sarah, a woman who rarely speaks, looks up at me with sudden clarity in her eyes. "I...I remember things. Terrible things. But they told me they were just nightmares."

"They're not nightmares," I say, kneeling beside her. "They're memories. We need to gather them, document them. We can bring this place down, but only if we work together."

As I speak, a surge of energy coursing through me. It's as if the very walls of Crossroads are listening, vibrating with the potential for change. For the first time in years, I feel truly alive, burning with purpose.

"It won't be easy," I warn them, my gaze sweeping across the room. "We'll face horrors beyond imagination. But we've already survived so much. Are you with me?"

There's a moment of heavy silence, and I fear I've misjudged. Then, slowly, hands raise. Nods of agreement. Whispered words of support.

As I look at their faces—some determined, some terrified, all bearing the scars of this place—I know our path forward will be treacherous. But for the first time since I arrived at Crossroads, a flicker of hope.

"Then let's begin," I say, my voice steady despite the storm of emotions within me. "It's time to tear down these walls and let the light in."

Chapter Eighteen

The darkness swallows me whole as I jolt awake, my heart a frantic bird in my chest. Shadows writhe on the crumbling walls of my asylum room, whispering secrets I can't—or don't want to—understand. I clutch my head, willing the cacophony of voices to cease.

"Stop," I plead, my voice a ragged whisper. "Please, just stop."

The voices only grow louder, a discordant symphony of pain and madness. I squeeze my eyes shut, but the darkness behind my lids offers no respite. Images flash rapid fire: scalpels glinting in harsh fluorescent light, restraints biting into pale flesh, screams echoing down endless corridors.

Are these memories or nightmares?

I force my eyes open, desperate to anchor myself. But reality in Crossroads Asylum is a fickle thing, as insubstantial as smoke.

The shadows on the walls commingle, forming grotesque figures that dance and cavort in a lurid ballet. I watch, transfixed, as they reach out with grasping tendrils.

"You can't elude us, Abigale," they seem to hiss. "You belong to the darkness now."

I shake my head violently, tangled hair whipping across my face. "No," I growl, surprising myself with the vehemence in my voice. "I don't belong to anyone."

An icy wind gusts through the room, carrying the stench of decay. The tattered curtains billow like specters, I swear I see faces in their folds—anguished, pleading faces of those long dead.

My gaze darts around the room, searching for something solid, something real. But even the familiar objects seem alien now. The rickety chair in the corner slides across the floor of its accord, its wooden legs scraping against the floorboards like nails on a chalkboard.

"It's all in my head." I whisper, convincing myself.

But if it's all in my head, why does everything feel so viscerally, terrifyingly real?

The whispering grows to a fever pitch, a thousand voices clamoring for attention. I catch snippets of conversation, disjointed phrases that make my blood run cold.

"The experiment was a success..."

"The subject shows remarkable resilience."

"Increase the dosage..."

My hands shake as I press them against my ears, but it does nothing to block out the noise. The shadows on the walls stretch and twist, forming a horrific tableau of torture and experimentation.

"What did you do to me?" I scream, my voice raw with fear and fury. "What am I?"

In response, the room seems to pulse, the very air thick with electric energy. Objects levitate—books, pens, my threadbare blanket—all swirling in a vortex of impossible motion.

I curl into myself, making my body as small as possible. There's no escape from the maelstrom of paranormal activity surrounding me. Every shadow, every whisper, every inexplicable movement hammers home a grim truth:

I am trapped in a nightmare and wondering if I'll ever wake up.

I lunge for the door, my fingers trembling as they grasp the numbing metal handle. The corridor beyond yawns before me, a pitch-black maw threatening to swallow me whole. My heart thunders in my chest as I take my first tentative step into the darkness.

"Keep it together, Abi," I mutter, willing my legs to move. "One foot in front of the other."

The air in the hallway is thick, heavy, as if the very walls are breathing. Each step I take echoes ominously, the sound bouncing off the dilapidated walls. Shadows dance at the edge of my vision, always just out of sight.

"Is anyone there?" I call out, my voice barely above a whisper. The silence that follows is deafening.

I press on, my hand trailing along the wall for guidance. The rough texture beneath my fingertips changes suddenly, becoming slick and warm. I recoil, my stomach churning.

"What's happening to me?" I wonder aloud, my voice quavering. "Am I losing my mind?"

A flicker of movement catches my eye. At the far end of the corridor, a figure darts across my field of vision, there and gone in an instant.

"Wait!" I cry out, desperation overriding my fear. "Please, I need help!"

I break into a run, my bare feet slapping against the cold floor. The world around me blurs, the shadows seeming to reach out with grasping fingers.

Suddenly, a blood-curdling scream pierces the air, stopping me dead in my tracks. It's a sound of pure anguish, raw and primal, emanating from a nearby room.

"Oh God," I whimper, my body trembling uncontrollably. "What was that?"

Every instinct yells at me to run, to find somewhere to hide. But a morbid curiosity takes hold, an inexplicable pull towards the source of that haunting cry.

"I have to know," I whisper, steeling myself. "I have to understand what's happening here."

With shaking hands, I reach for the door handle, taking a deep breath, close my eyes, and push it open, stepping into the unknown.

I step into a turbulence of chaos. The room before me is a nightmare made manifest, furniture strewn about as if tossed by a violent tempest. A chair lies splintered in the corner, its broken legs accusingly pointed towards the ceiling. The remnants of a desk are scattered across the floor, papers strewn like fallen leaves.

"What happened here?" I gasp, my eyes darting frantically around the room.

It's the walls that truly capture my attention, stealing the breath from my lungs. Every inch is covered in cryptic symbols and frenzied writings, etched by an unseen hand. I approach, squinting in the dim light to make out the words.

"The shadows whisper...they know... they always know," I read aloud, my voice barely above a whisper.

A chill runs down my spine as I realize the writing is still fresh, glistening wetly in the pale moonlight filtering through the barred window. My fingers trace the nearest symbol, coming away stained with a dark, sticky substance.

"Is this...blood?" I choke out, bile rising in my throat.

The air grows heavy, pressing down on me like a physical weight. The hairs on the back of my neck stand on end, and I'm overcome with the overwhelming sensation of being watched.

"Who's there?" I call out, my voice trembling. "Show yourself!"

Only silence answers, but the feeling of an unseen presence intensifies. My mind races, struggling to make sense of what I'm experiencing. Are these paranormal phenomena real, or am I finally losing my grip on reality?

"This can't be happening," I mutter, pressing my palms against my temples. "The experiments, the asylum...it's all in my head, isn't it?"

But as I turn to flee, my eyes catch a flickering movement in the shattered remains of a mirror. For just a moment, I see a face that isn't mine staring back at me, its eyes hollow and filled with an ancient sorrow.

"Oh God," I whimper, backing away. "What am I becoming?"

The shadows in the corridor seem to writhe and twist as I stumble out of the room, my heart pounding in my chest. Each step feels like wading through molasses, the air thick with an energy that threatens to suffocate me.

"Leave me alone!" I cry out, my voice echoing off the walls.

A whisper caresses my ear, so close I can feel phantom lips against my skin. "Abigale...stay... with us..."

I whirl around, but there's nothing there except the endless, dimly lit hallway. As I turn back, a figure flickers at the edge of my vision, there and gone in an instant.

"This isn't real," I mutter, clenching my fists, so tightly my nails dig into my palms. "You're not real!"

But the whispers grow louder, a ring of voices overlapping until I can't distinguish individual words. Shadows dance along the walls, reaching out with tendrils of darkness that seem to grasp at my clothes, my hair, my very soul.

I break into a run, my bare feet slapping against the cold floor. "I need to find somewhere safe," I pant, my eyes darting frantically from side to side.

As if answering my unspoken prayer, I spot a familiar wooden door at the end of the hall. The asylum's chapel. Without hesitation, I lunge for the handle and throw myself inside.

Chapter Nineteen

The heavy door slams shut behind me, cutting off the whispers mid-sentence. I lean against it, gasping for breath, before slowly turning to face the chapel's interior.

"Oh," I breathe, my eyes widening at the sight before me.

A row of candles flickers along the altar, their warm light a stark contrast to the stifling darkness of the asylum. Yet even here, shadows play along the walls, twisting the crucifix's silhouette into grotesque shapes.

I take a tentative step forward; the floorboards creaking ominously beneath my feet. "Hello?" I call out, my voice small in the cavernous space. "Is anyone here?"

Only the guttering of the candles answers me, but the air feels heavy with anticipation, as if the very walls are holding their breath.

I approach the altar, my steps echoing in the stillness. The flickering candlelight dances across my face as I sink to my knees, clasping my trembling hands together.

"Please," I whisper, my voice cracking. "If anyone's listening...I need help. I don't understand what's happening to me."

As the words leave my lips, a chill ripples through the air. The candles sputter and, in an instant, extinguish as one.

My heart pounds against my rib cage. "No," I breathe, fear clawing its way up my throat. "No, no, no..."

That's when I feel it—a presence behind me, looming. A cold breath tickles my nape, raising goosebumps along my skin.

I want to scream, but terror has frozen my vocal cords. My mind races, fragments of thoughts colliding. Is this another hallucination? Or is it real? God, what if it's real?

"Who's there?" I choke out, my voice barely above a whisper.

The presence doesn't respond, but it's drawing closer, the cold intensifying. My instincts scream at me to run, to flee, to escape this nightmare.

Blindly, I lurch to my feet, spinning around. In the pitch darkness, I glimpse something—a pair of glowing eyes, filled with an otherworldly hunger.

"Stay away!" I shriek, stumbling backward. My hip collides with the altar, sending pain shooting through my body, but I hardly notice. All I can focus on is escape.

I turn and run, my hands outstretched in the darkness, desperately seeking the door. Behind me, I hear movement—a rustling, a scraping, the sound of something inhuman giving chase.

My fingers brush the wood, and I sob with relief as I find the door handle. I wrench it open and burst into the corridor, not daring to look back.

I careen through the asylum's winding corridors, my breath coming in ragged gasps. The shadows seem alive, reaching for me with spectral fingers. My mind reels, struggling to process the horrors I've witnessed.

"This can't be real," I mutter, my voice hoarse. "It can't be."

I round a corner and skid to a halt. Before me stands a door, I've never seen this one before either, like they're manifesting out of the building, its wood warped and paint peeling. It calls to me, a whisper in the recesses of my fractured psyche.

My trembling hand reaches for the rusted doorknob. It turns with a groan, and I stumble into a room that seems frozen in time.

"Oh my...," I breathe, taking in the scene before me.

Ancient medical equipment looms in the shadows—a dentist's chair with rusted restraints, shelves lined with cloudy jars containing God-knows-what. The air is thick with dust and the acrid scent of decay.

My gaze falls on a filing cabinet in the corner, its drawers slightly ajar. Drawn by an inexplicable compulsion, I approach it, my fingers trailing through the dust on its surface.

I pull open the top drawer, wincing at the screech. Inside, I find a collection of manila folders, each bearing a name. My heart nearly stops when I see my own: "Sheetz, Abigale."

With trembling hands, I extract the file and open it. The first page is a photograph—a younger version of myself, eyes vacant, strapped to that very chair across the room.

"No," I whisper, bile rising in my throat. "This can't be real."

As I read on, memories surface—fractured, ghastly glimpses of experiments, of pain, of voices urging me to unlock a hidden part of myself.

I sink to the floor, clutching the file to my chest. "Am I going mad?" I wonder aloud, my voice echoing in the empty room. "Or have I always been?"

The shadows seem to whisper in response, and I squeeze my eyes shut, blocking out the world around me. But the terrors persist, leaving me to question everything I thought I knew about myself and this asylum that has become my prison.

I'm about to leave the room, my legs shaking as I hear a faint whisper stopping me cold. It's coming from within the walls, a sound like dry leaves scraping against stone.

"Abigale," it hisses, my name elongated into a sinister caress. "The truth lies beneath."

I whirl around, heart pounding. "Who's there?" My voice cracks, betraying my fear.

The whisper continues, its tone a mix of seduction and menace. "We've been waiting for you, child of shadows. The asylum hungers. It feeds on secrets...and pain."

A chill runs down my spine. "What do you mean? What secrets?"

"Look deeper," it urges. "The experiments were just the beginning. Crossroads are more than bricks and mortar. It's alive, Abigale. And you...you are its chosen one."

I press my hands against my ears, blocking out the voice. "No, you're not real. This is merely another hallucination."

But even as I deny it, something shifts within me. A resolve, born of desperation and determination, takes root.

"I won't be a victim anymore," I declare, my voice growing stronger. "If this place is alive, if these horrors are real, then I'll face them. I'll uncover every dark secret, every hidden truth."

The whisper fades, leaving behind an eerie silence. I straighten my spine, clenching my fists at my sides.

"Do you hear me, Crossroads?" I call out, my words echoing through the empty corridors. "I'm coming for you. For all of you who hurt me, who hurt others. Your reign of terror ends now."

With newfound purpose, I stride out of the room, ready to confront whatever nightmares await me in the depths of this asylum. The shadows may whisper, the walls may bleed, but I am no longer afraid. I am Abigale Sheetz, and I will bring this house of horrors crumbling down.

I stride down the dimly lit corridor, my heart pounding in my chest. The flickering lights cast grotesque shadows on the crumbling walls, and I can't shake the feeling that they're reaching for me. Suddenly, the air grows colder, and a mist coalesces at the end of the hall.

"Who's there?" I call out, my voice trembling despite my resolve.

The mist swirls and takes shape, forming into a translucent figure. It's a woman, her form ethereal and shimmering. Her eyes, pools of sorrow and longing, lock onto mine. She raises a spectral hand, beckoning me forward.

I hesitate, my legs refusing to move. "Are you...are you real?"

The figure doesn't speak, but a pull, an inexplicable urge to approach. My curiosity wars with my fear, each step a battle between my instinct for self-preservation and my desperate need for answers.

"What do you want from me?" I whisper, taking a tentative step forward. The ghost's eyes seem to brighten, a flicker of hope amidst the sadness.

My mind races. Is this another trick of the asylum? Another cruel experiment designed to break me? Or could this specter be the key to unlocking the secrets that have haunted me for so long?

"I'm not afraid of you," I lie, my voice stronger than I feel. "If you have something to show me, then show me."

The ghost's form wavers, and for a moment, it might disappear. But then it solidifies, and I see a tear roll down its translucent cheek. It turns slightly, still beckoning, as if inviting me to follow.

I take another step, and another. My heart thunders in my ears, drowning out the ever-present whispers of the asylum. "Where are you leading me?" I ask, but receive no answer.

As I draw closer, I can make out more details of the spectral woman. Her clothes are old-fashioned, reminiscent of a bygone era. There's something familiar about her face, a nagging sensation that I should recognize her.

"Do I...do I know you?" I breathe, now just a few feet away from the apparition.

The ghost's lips move, but no sound comes out. Yet somehow, I understand. She's telling me something, something vital. I reach out, my fingers trembling, inching closer to her outstretched hand.

"What is it?" I plead. "What do you need me to know?"

Just as my fingertips are about to contact the ghostly form, a distant scream echoes through the asylum. The apparition's eyes widen in fear, and she fades.

"No, wait!" I cry out, lunging forward. "Don't go!"

But it's too late. The ghost vanishes, leaving me alone in the dark corridor, my hand grasping at empty air. I'm left with more questions than answers, and a growing certainty that the asylum's secrets run deeper than I ever imagined.

Chapter Twenty
POV Warden

The shadows in Dr. Harker's office seem to writhe and twist as I burst through the door, my footsteps echoing like thunderclaps in the eerie silence. The air is thick with the scent of old books and something darker, more sinister.

"Dr. Harker," I growl, my voice low and taut with barely contained fury. "We need to talk about Abigale."

The doctor looks up from his desk, his piercing eyes meeting mine with cold indifference. "Warden Mitchell," he drawls, "to what do I owe this...intrusion?"

I clench my fists, feeling my nails dig into my palms. "The experiments, doctor. They've gone too far. The brutality is escalating beyond acceptable limits."

Dr. Harker's lips curl into a smirk that sends a chill down my spine. "Acceptable limits? And who, pray tell, decides what those limits are?"

"I do," I snap, drawing myself up to my full height. "As warden of this asylum, I have a duty to protect-"

"Protect?" Dr. Harker interrupts, his voice dripping with disdain. "Your duty, Warden, is to facilitate progress. And progress often requires...sacrifices."

My stomach churns at his casual cruelty. "But Abigale-"

"Is a necessary part of my research," he cuts me off again, rising from his chair with fluid grace. "My work here could revolutionize our understanding of the human mind. Surely, you can see the value in that?"

I falter, my resolve wavering under the weight of his words. "But at what cost?" I whisper, more to myself than to him.

Dr. Harker's eyes gleam with a fervor that borders on madness. "Any cost, Warden. For the advancement of science, any cost is justified."

As we face off in the dimly lit office, I can't shake the feeling that I'm staring into the abyss itself.

— Abigale

In a small, dank room not far away, I press my ear against the cold, unforgiving wall. My heart pounds so loudly I fear it might drown out the muffled voices seeping through the thin barrier. Warden Mitchell's gruff tones clash with Dr. Harker's silky cadence, their words indistinct but their emotions palpable.

Hope flutters in my chest like a trapped bird. Is the Warden fighting for me? Dare someone in this hellish place care about my fate?

As I strain to make out their words, fear coils around my heart, squeezing mercilessly. What if the Warden fails? What if Dr. Harker's influence is too strong?

I close my eyes, willing myself to hear more, to understand. My fingers trace the rough texture of the wall, as if I could somehow reach through it and grasp the truth on the other side.

"Please," I whisper, my voice barely audible even to my own ears. "Please help me."

But the voices continue their muffled dance, oblivious to my desperate pleas, and I'm left alone with my pounding heart and the terrifying uncertainty of what comes next.

Dr. Harker's voice suddenly rises, sharp and venomous. "I've had enough of your meddling, Mitchell. One more word about my methods, and I'll ensure your superiors learn of your...obstructive tendencies."

The threat hangs in the air, thick and suffocating. I press myself closer to the wall, desperate to catch every word.

"You can't—" Warden Mitchell starts, his voice faltering.

"Oh, but I can," Dr. Harker interrupts, his words dripping with malice. "Who do you think they'll believe? The decorated scientist pushing boundaries, or a warden with a guilty conscience?"

Silence follows, heavy and obtrusive. I imagine Warden Mitchell's face, his stern features contorted in an internal struggle. My hands ball into fists, nails digging crescents into my palms. Please, are tenacious. Not now.

"I...understand," Warden Mitchell finally says, his voice hollow. "Continue with your work, Doctor."

The weight of those words crashes over me like a tidal wave of despair. My legs buckle, and I slide down the wall, my body trembling uncontrollably.

"No," I whisper, tears welling in my eyes. "No, no, no."

The cold, hard floor beneath me offers no comfort as I curl into myself, sobs wracking my frail frame. The last ember of hope flickers and dies, leaving me in utter darkness.

I'm truly alone again now, abandoned in this nightmare. The walls of my tiny room seem to close in, mocking my helplessness. Tears stream down my face, each one a testament to my shattered spirit.

"Why?" I choke out between sobs. "Why won't anyone help me?"

But only the empty silence of Crossroads Asylum answers, echoing with the ghosts of countless others who have suffered within these cursed walls. And I know, with a bone-deep certainty, that my torment has only just begun.

The door creaks open, and Dr. Harker's shadow falls across me like a shroud. I look up, my tear-stained face contorting in terror as I see the chilling smile that plays across his lips. His eyes, cold and calculating, bore into mine as he steps into the room.

"Abigale," he purrs, his voice dripping with false sweetness. "I have wonderful news. We're going to push the boundaries of science even further."

I scramble backwards, pressing myself against the wall. "No," I whisper, my voice hoarse. "Please, no more."

Dr. Harker's smile widens. "Oh, but we've only scratched the surface. Your mind, your body — they hold such potential. We're going to unlock it all."

He approaches, looming over me. I can smell antiseptic and something metallic on his breath. My heart hammers against my ribs, threatening to burst from my chest.

"Come now," he says, reaching for me. "Let's not waste any more time."

His hands are on me, cold and unyielding. I thrash, breaking free, but he's too strong. "Stop!" I scream, my voice echoing off the walls. "You can't do this!"

Dr. Harker chuckles, the sound sending ice through my veins. "But I can, Abigale. And I will."

He drags me to the metal table in the center of the room. I dig my heels in, fighting with every ounce of strength I have left. But it's futile. Within moments, I'm on my back, leather straps biting into my wrists and ankles.

"Please," I beg, tears streaming down my face. "I'm not strong enough. You'll break me."

Chapter Twenty-One

Dr. Harker leans over me, his face inches from mine. His eyes gleam with a sadistic glee that turns my stomach. "That's precisely the point, my dear. We'll break you down to build you up anew. Isn't science marvelous?"

I close my eyes, shutting out his face, his voice, this entire nightmare. But I can still feel his presence, hear the soft clink of metal instruments being arranged nearby. And I know that no matter how tightly I squeeze my eyes shut, I can't escape the horror that's about to unfold.

The world goes dark as Dr. Harker slips a thick blindfold over my eyes. I gasp, my other senses instantly heightening. The antiseptic smell of the room burns my nostrils. Every sound—the hum of machinery, Dr. Harker's measured breathing, my own panicked heartbeat—crashes against my eardrums like waves in a storm.

"Sensory deprivation," Dr. Harker explains, his voice unnervingly calm, "combined with targeted electrical stimulation. We're going to rewire that fascinating brain of yours, Abigale."

Cold electrodes being pressed against my temples. My breath comes in ragged gasps. "You can't...you can't do this," I stammer, my words sounding hollow even in my own ears.

"Nonsense," he replies. "Watch me...Oh, you can't," he smirks.

A switch flips, and suddenly, my world explodes into pain. White-hot agony sears through my skull, setting every nerve ending ablaze. I scream, the sound tearing from my throat and echoing through the asylum's cavernous halls.

"Fascinating," I hear Dr. Harker murmur, his voice barely audible over the buzzing electricity and my own anguished cries. "Your resilience is truly remarkable."

The pain intensifies, and I find myself slipping. My thoughts scatter like leaves in a gale. Who am I? Where does Abigale end and the pain begin? I cling desperately to memories—my name, my past—but they crumble like ash in my mental grasp.

"Stop," I whimper, but if the word leaves my lips, it's lost in the ether of space, "Please...I'm losing... me."

Dr. Harker's reply comes from far away, distorted as if underwater. "That's the point, my dear. Let go. Embrace the chaos."

Another wave of electricity courses through me, I shatter, my consciousness splintering into a thousand glittering shards. I'm falling, drowning, burning—all at once. The line between reality and nightmare blurs, leaving me afloat in an ocean of terror and confusion.

In this limbo of fractured thoughts and searing pain, a small part of me wonders if I'll ever find my way back to myself again.

Dr. Harker's face swims into view, his dark eyes gleaming with cruel satisfaction. "You're weakening, Abigale," he taunts, his words slicing through the haze of my agony. "How does it feel to be so utterly powerless?"

I try to speak, to scream, to fight back, my body betrays me. My muscles spasm uncontrollably, every nerve ending aflame. I'm a puppet, and he holds the strings.

"Your mind is an open book to me now," he continues, adjusting a dial on the machine beside me. The buzzing intensifies, and I feel my back arch involuntarily. "Every secret, every fear...all mine to explore."

Through the fog of pain, a thought surfaces: I am more than this. I am not just his experiment. But the words dissolve before I can grasp them fully.

Dr. Harker leans closer, his breath hot on my ear. "You're breaking beautifully, my dear. Soon, you'll be reborn."

Another jolt of electricity courses through me, more intense than before. My vision blurs, dark spots dancing at the edges. I know dimly that I'm convulsing violently now, my body pushed beyond its limits.

"Please," I gasp between involuntary jerks. "I can't...I'm..."

Consciousness is slipping away, dragging me into a void darker than any I've known. As I teeter on the brink, one last thought flickers through my fading mind:

I will survive this. I must.

Then, mercifully, everything goes black.

The acrid smell of ozone and burnt hair assaults my nostrils as consciousness sluggishly returns. My eyelids flutter open, struggling against the weight of exhaustion. Dr. Harker's face swims into focus above me, his eyes gleaming with a mixture of satisfaction and barely contained excitement.

"Welcome back, Abigale," he says, his voice dripping with false concern. "I was worried we'd pushed too far."

I'd respond, but my throat feels raw, scraped clean by my own screams. Only a weak rasp escapes my lips.

Dr. Harker's lips curl into a cruel smile. "Oh, don't strain yourself. We've made remarkable progress today." He removes the electrodes from my temples, his touch clinical and devoid of any genuine care. "This is just the beginning. The worst, my dear, is yet to come."

His words send a chill through my battered body. What could be worse than this? I wonder, terror clawing at the edges of my mind.

"Rest now," he says, moving towards the door. "You'll need your strength for what lies ahead."

The heavy metal door clangs shut behind him, leaving me alone in the smothering silence of the room. I remain motionless on the cold table, my muscles twitching sporadically, aftershocks of the torture I've endured.

My gaze fixed on a crack in the ceiling, a jagged line stretching across the dingy white paint. It becomes my anchor as my thoughts spiral, fragments of memories and fears swirling in a dizzying kaleidoscope.

This can't be the end, clinging desperately to a thread of defiance. There must be a way out. I just need to find it.

Tears leak from the corners of my eyes, trailing down my temples and into my matted hair. But even as despair threatens to engulf me, a tiny spark ignites deep within my chest. It's fragile, barely more than a whisper, but it's there:

Hope.

I will escape this nightmare, I vow silently. Somehow, someway, I will be free.

Chapter Twenty-Two

The world spins and fractures, kaleidoscopic fragments of reality shattering around me. My vision blurs, colors bleeding into one another like watercolors on wet paper. The asylum's dim corridors stretch and warp, twisting into impossible geometries that defy logic. Every sound echoes with painful clarity—the distant drip of water, the skittering of unseen creatures in the walls, the ragged whisper of my breath.

"Where am I?" I gasp, my voice sounding alien and distorted to my own ears. My fingers brush against the disintegrating.

wallpaper, the texture suddenly overwhelming, each fiber distinct and alive beneath my hypersensitive skin.

A chill wind whips through the corridor, carrying with it the musty scent of decay and abandonment. The surrounding shadows deepen, coalescing into a dark, amorphous figure. Piercing eyes gleam from the inky blackness, pinning me in place with their intensity.

"Poor, lonely Abigale," a haunting voice echoes from the depths of the shadow. "Always left behind, always forgotten."

I stumble backward, heart pounding. "No, that's not true. I'm not alone."

The shadow laughs, a chilling sound that reverberates through my bones. "Aren't you? Where are your friends now? Your family? Even the other patients avoid you."

Memories flood my mind unbidden—faces of those I once cared for, blurring, and fading like photographs left too long in the sun. I shake my head violently, dispelling the images. "Stop it! They didn't abandon me. I'm here to help them."

"Help them?" the shadow mocks. "You can't even help yourself. You're trapped here, just like the rest of us. Forgotten. Discarded."

I press my palms against my temples, willing the voice to stop. But it persists, a relentless whisper in the back of my mind. "No one is coming for you, Abigale. No one cares."

"That's not true," I insist, even as doubt gnaws at the edges of my conviction. "I'll find a way out. I'll expose the truth about this place."

The shadow seems to grow, looming over me. "And who will believe the ravings of a madwoman? You'll die here, alone and not mourned."

I squeeze my eyes shut, blocking out the taunting voice and the twisting, surreal landscape around me. But in the darkness behind my eyelids, I see only abandonment and isolation stretching endlessly before me.

With a sudden surge of clarity, I open my eyes and confront the shadow directly. "You're wrong," I snarl, my voice raw doggedly. "I'm stronger than you think."

The shadow flickers, momentarily taken aback by my defiance. I press on, "I've survived this long, haven't I? Through all their experiments, their manipulations. I'm still here."

"But for how long?" it hisses, its form undulating like smoke.

"As long as it takes," I retort, clenching my fists. "I won't let you or this place break me."

The shadow lunges forward, its inky tendrils reaching for me. But I stand my ground, feeling a surge of power coursing through my veins. "You're just a manifestation of my fear," I declare. "You have no actual power over me."

As I speak these words, the shadow begins to dissipate, wisps of darkness curling away into nothingness. I exhale sharply, a mixture of relief and triumph washing over me.

But my victory is short-lived.

The air around me shimmers, and I find myself face-to-face with...myself. Or rather, a twisted version of myself. My ghostly double of a living person's features are contorted, eyes sunken and skin sallow. Its lips curl into a sneer as it speaks with my voice, but filled with venom.

"Well, well," it drawls. "Look who thinks she's so strong now."

I recoil, my heart pounding. This new demon is more terrifying than the last, its familiarity a perversion of everything I am.

"You think you've won something?" it continues, circling me. "You're still trapped here, still responsible for every life you've ruined."

I shake my head, dispelling its words, but they sink into me like poison. "I have ruined no lives," I whisper, but my voice lacks conviction.

The demon laughs, a harsh, grating sound. "Oh, really? What about the orderly you attacked last month? Or the other patients you've dragged into your delusions?"

Memories flash through my mind–faces twisted in fear, accusations hurled at me. I struggle to differentiate between reality and the asylum's manipulations.

"That's not...I didn't mean to..." I stammer, my newfound strength wavering in the face of this onslaught of guilt.

The demon's eyes flash with cruel delight. "Of course you didn't mean to. You never do, do you, Abigale? You're always the victim, never responsible for your actions."

I clench my fists, nails digging into my palms. "That's not true," I hiss, but doubt gnaws at me.

"Isn't it?" The demon's voice drips with sarcasm. "Tell me, how many lives have you touched here at Crossroads? How many have you tainted with your madness?"

Images flood my mind–other patients cowering from me, nurses whispering behind their hands. The weight of guilt threatens to crush me.

"I...I was just surviving," I whisper, my voice cracking.

The demon leans in close, its breath hot on my ear. "At what cost, Abigale? At what cost?"

I close my eyes, fighting against the tide of self-loathing. "No," I say, my voice growing stronger. "I won't let you twist this. I've made mistakes, I'm not the monster you're painting me as."

The demon snarls, its form flickering. "You can't escape your guilt that easily."

"I'm not eluding it," I counter, meeting its gaze. "I'm accepting it. And I'm choosing to forgive myself."

As I speak the words, something shift within me. The demon howls in frustration, its form beginning to dissolve.

But before I can savor this small victory, the surrounding air thickens. A new presence emerges, monstrous and multi-limbed, its eyes gleaming with malevolent intelligence.

"Oh, Abigale," it purrs, its voice a cacophony of whispers. "Do you really think you're in control here?"

The creature's limbs writhe around me, each one a grasping tendril of chaos. I can feel its influence seeping into my mind, a maelstrom of conflicting impulses and desires.

"Get out of my head!" I scream, clawing at my scalp. My nails dig into flesh, drawing blood, but the pain helps me focus.

The demon laughs, a sound like shattering glass. "But I am your head, Abigale. I'm every dark thought you've ever suppressed, every wild impulse you've denied."

I grit my teeth, forcing myself to stand straight despite the vertigo threatening to topple me. "You're wrong. I'm more than my impulses."

"Are you?" it taunts. One of its limbs lashes out, wrapping around my throat. "Then why did you hurt that orderly last week? Why did you scream at the kind nurse who only wanted to help?"

Memories flash before my eyes–my hands lashing out, my voice raised in anger. But I push past them, focusing on the present.

"Because I was scared," I admit, my voice hoarse but steady. "But fear doesn't control me anymore."

I grab the limb around my throat, ignoring the burning sensation as I pry it away. "I choose who I aspire to be. Not you, not Dr. Harker, not anyone else."

The demon shrieks, its form wavering. "You can't resist forever!"

"I don't need to," I counter, standing taller. "Just long enough to win."

As I speak, a surge of strength. The chaos in my mind recedes, replaced by a clarity I haven't felt in years.

But as the third demon fades, darkness closes in. It's thick, tangible, pressing against my skin and seeping into my lungs.

"No..." I gasp, struggling to breathe as the blackness envelops me. "Not again..."

The suffocating presence whispers in my ear, its voice a frigid wind of despair. "Welcome back to your cage, Abigale. Did you really think you could escape?"

I claw at the darkness, my fingers passing through inky tendrils that cling to my skin like tar. The walls of Crossroads seem to close in, the peeling wallpaper and rusted fixtures morphing into prison bars.

"You're trapped," the darkness hisses. "Forever confined in this asylum, powerless to change your fate."

My chest tightens, panic rising. But somewhere deep within, a spark of defiance ignites.

"No," I growl, pushing against the crushing weight. "I've survived worse than you."

I close my eyes, focusing on memories of strength—standing up to bullies as a child, enduring Dr. Harker's "treatments," fighting my way through each demon.

"I may be trapped here physically," I say, my voice growing stronger, "but my mind is my own."

The darkness recoils slightly, and I press on. "Every day I choose to keep fighting. That's not powerlessness—that's strength."

A tiny pinprick of light appears, growing brighter as I concentrate on it. The demon shrieks, its form dissipating around the edges.

"You can't erase me that easily," it snarls, but there's a note of uncertainty in its voice.

I reach out, grasping the light. As warmth spreads through my fingers, realization dawns.

"You're all connected, aren't you?" I murmur, pieces clicking into place. "Each of you — abandonment, guilt, loss of control, confinement — your fragments of my past."

The light pulses, and I see flashes of memory: my parents' rejection, mistakes I've agonized over, moments of helplessness in the asylum.

"But you're not all of me," I breathe. "You're just the wounds I need to heal."

The realization crashes over me like a tidal wave, leaving me gasping. My knees buckle and I sink to the cold, damp floor of my cell. The truth I've been running from for so long stands stark before me, impossible to ignore.

"It was all him," I whisper, my voice trembling. "Dr. Harker...he's been orchestrating this nightmare from the beginning."

Memories flood in, no longer fragmented but painfully clear. The endless "treatments," the drugs, the manipulation—all designed to break me down, to reshape my mind into his twisted vision.

"You bastard," I snarl, anger swelling within me. "You made me doubt my sanity!"

My fists clench so tightly my nails dig into my palms, drawing blood. The pain grounds me, reminds me I'm still here, still fighting.

"Abigale," a silky voice echoes from the corridor. Dr. Harker. "Are you ready for our next session?"

I freeze, terror and rage warring within me. But beneath it all, a cold determination takes root.

"I'm coming for you," I whisper, too softly for him to hear. "I'll expose everything you've done."

As his footsteps draw nearer, I force myself to stand. My legs shake, but I lock my knees, refusing to show weakness.

The cell door creaks open, and Dr. Harker's piercing eyes meet mine. For a moment, I see a flicker of surprise—he wasn't expecting to find me standing, defiant.

"Well," he says, his tone deceptively light. "We've made some progress today. Shall we continue our work?"

I nod, not trusting myself to speak. As he leads me down the shadowy corridor, my mind races. How can I gather evidence? Who can I trust? The enormity of the task before me is daunting, but I cling to my newfound clarity.

I'll bring the truth to light. And when I do, Crossroads Asylum will crumble, taking Dr. Harker's twisted legacy with it.

Chapter Twenty-Three

The moonlight slices through the cracked window, casting anemic shadows across Dr. Harker's office. My heart pounds in my ears as I ease the door shut behind me, wincing at the faint click of the latch. The room smells of stale coffee and something metallic—like old pennies or dried blood.

"You shouldn't be here," a voice whispers. I whirl around, but the office is empty. Just another phantom speaking from the recesses of my fractured mind.

I creep toward the hulking mahogany desk, my fingers trailing over its polished surface. "Where are you hiding your secrets, Doctor?" I murmur, pulling open the top drawer. Nothing but pens and paperclips.

My hands tremble as I rifle through stacks of patient files, the faces of the lost and broken staring up at me from glossy photographs. So many lives touched by his "care." I shudder, remembering the sting of needles and the acrid taste of pills forced down my throat.

A floorboard creaks in the hallway. I freeze, holding my breath as footsteps approach. Please, not now. Not when I'm so close. The steps fade, and I exhale shakily.

"Keep looking," the phantom voice urges. "He can't hide the truth forever."

I nod, though no one is there to see. My fingers probe the underside of the desk, searching for hidden latches or compartments. Nothing. I slump in Dr. Harker's chair, defeat washing over me.

"Think, Abigale," I mutter. "Where would a monster keep his darkest secrets?"

My gaze drifts to the imposing bookcase lining the far wall. Of course. I hurry over, scanning the dusty tomes. One stands out—a thick volume on cognitive neuroscience. When I tug it free, a soft click echoes in the silence.

A hidden drawer slides open, revealing a stack of manila folders. My hands shake as I lift them out, spreading the contents across the desk. Charts, diagrams, and pages of meticulous notes detailing experiments. My experiments.

"Oh God," I breathe, bile rising in my throat. "What has he done to me?"

My eyes dart across the pages, devouring every horrifying detail. Each word is a dagger, piercing through the fragile illusion of safety I'd constructed. Dr. Harker's neat handwriting mocks me as I read:

"Subject A.S. displays remarkable psychic potential. Increased doses of Compound X-27 have yielded promising results. Further testing required to push cognitive boundaries."

I clench my fists, crumpling the paper. "I'm not your lab rat," I hiss through gritted teeth.

The room spins as I continue reading, piecing together the sinister puzzle of my existence here. Memories flood back—flashes of pain, disorientation, and terror. All carefully orchestrated by the man I trusted to help me.

"He never wanted to cure you," the phantom voice whispers. "He wanted to weaponize you."

My hands tremble violently as I flip through more documents. Blueprints for a device designed to amplify psychic abilities. Lists of potential "subjects" for future experiments. And there, at the bottom of the stack, a letter to a shadowy government agency, promising breakthroughs in mind control technology.

"No," I choke out, tears blurring my vision. "This can't be real."

But it is. The truth crashes over me like a tidal wave, leaving me gasping for air. Every kind word, every reassuring touch—all lies. Dr. Harker saw me not as a person to heal, but as a means to an end.

Rage bubbles up inside me, hot and dangerous. I want to scream, to tear this office apart with my bare hands. But beneath the anger, fear coils in my gut. What more has he done? What horrors await me if I don't escape?

"You have to stop him," the voice urges. "Before he does this to anyone else."

I nod, resolve hardening within me. "I will," I whisper, carefully replacing the documents. "Whatever it takes."

My fingers work methodically, arranging the papers exactly as I found them. Each motion is deliberate, measured—a stark contrast to the chaos raging within me. The office, once a sanctuary, now feels like a trap closing in. I can almost hear the ticking of an unseen clock, counting down the moments until my betrayal is discovered.

"Hurry," I mutter to myself, sliding the last file into place. "He could return any minute."

With trembling hands, I ease the drawer shut, wincing at the soft click it makes, only taking the one picture. My eyes dart to the door, half-expecting to see Dr. Harker's silhouette looming there. But the hallway remains empty, silent save for the pounding of my heart.

I take a deep breath, steadying myself. "Focus, Abigale," I whisper. "You know where he'll be."

The basement. That's where Dr. Harker conducts his most insidious work. I've caught glimpses of it before—sterile tables, strange machines, the acrid smell of chemicals. Now, armed with the truth, those fragments coalesce into a horrifying picture.

As I slip out of the office, a chill runs down my spine. The familiar corridors of Crossroads seem alien now, every shadow concealing a threat. My bare feet make no sound on the cold floor as I move towards the stairwell.

"What if he catches you?" the ever-present voice in my mind asks.

I clench my fists, feeling a surge of defiance. "Then I'll make him pay for what he's done," I reply, my voice barely audible. "To me, and to who knows how many others."

The stairs loom before me, descending into darkness. Each step feels like a choice—to confront the monster who's manipulated me, or to flee back to the false safety of ignorance. But there's no going back now. I've seen behind the curtain, and I can't un-know the truth.

Taking a deep breath, I begin my descent into the depths of Crossroads Asylum, towards whatever nightmare awaits me below.

The basement air hits me like a damp shroud, heavy with decay and secrets. Dim bulbs flicker weakly along the corridor, struggling against the encroaching darkness. Each step echoes ominously, accompanied by the steady drip-drip-drip of water from unseen pipes.

"Left, or right?" I murmur, peering down the branching hallways. My mind races, fragments of memory flashing behind my eyes. I've been down here before, haven't I? In those hazy periods, I can never recall.

A distant clang startles me, and I press myself against the slimy wall, heart pounding. “It's just the pipes,” I reassure myself, but my voice quavers. “Get it together, Abi.”

I choose the right path, guided by an instinct I don't fully understand. The corridor twists and turns, a maze designed to disorient. Or to trap. With each step, the weight of what I'm about to do settles heavier on my shoulders.

“He'll have answers,” I whisper, clenching and unclenching my fists. “He has to.”

Finally, I spot it—a heavy metal door at the end of the hall. Even from here, I can feel the wrongness emanating from beyond. My legs feel leaden as I approach, memories of pain and violation threatening to overwhelm me.

I reach for the doorknob, my hand trembling violently. "This is it," I breathe, fingers hovering inches from the cold metal. "No turning back now."

For a moment, I'm frozen, caught between terror and determination. Then, steeling myself, I grasp the knob and turn.

Chapter Twenty-Four

The door creaks open, revealing a sterile nightmare. I step inside, my senses immediately assaulted by the harsh reality of Dr. Harker's twisted sanctuary.

Rows of gleaming medical equipment line the walls, their purpose as sinister as it is mysterious. Fluorescent lights flicker overhead, casting an otherworldly glow that makes my skin crawl. The air is thick with the cloying scent of antiseptic, threatening to choke me with memories of past "treatments."

"What fresh hell is this?" I whisper, my eyes darting from one horrific instrument to another.

In the center of the room stands Dr. Harker, his back to me as he hunches over a workbench. The sight of him ignites a fire in my chest, rage burning away the last vestiges of fear.

"You won't get away with this," I think, my hands clenching into fists. "Not anymore."

I take a step forward, the sound of my footfall impossibly loud in the oppressive silence. Dr. Harker doesn't turn, so engrossed in his work that he hasn't noticed my intrusion.

"What are you working on, doctor?" I call out, my voice steadier than I feel. "Another way to break minds, or just hearts, this time?"

My anger swells, a living thing clawing at my insides. The fluorescent lights above me pulse in sync with my racing heart, casting wild shadows across the room.

Dr. Harker's shoulders tense, but he doesn't turn. "Ah, Abigale," he says, his voice as cold and clinical as ever. "I wasn't expecting you. Come to volunteer for more... treatments?"

"I've come for the truth," I spit back, taking another step closer. "And this time, I won't let you twist it."

My voice quivers, a mix of fear and defiance coloring my words as I continue, "I know what you've done, Dr. Harker. The experiments, the manipulation... you've been using me as your personal lab rat."

The words taste like ash in my mouth, but I force them out, each accusation a small act of rebellion against the man who has controlled my reality for so long.

Dr. Harker turns slowly, his movements deliberate and unhurried. As he faces me, I see a sinister smile playing on his lips, a sight that sends a chill down my spine despite the anger burning in my chest.

"Oh, Abigale," he says, his voice dripping with false sympathy. "You speak as if what I've done is a cruelty, when in fact, it's the greatest kindness anyone has ever shown you."

I feel my rage intensify, threatening to consume me. "Kindness?" I spit out. "You call torturing me kindness?"

Dr. Harker's smile widens, his eyes gleaming with a fervor that makes my skin crawl. "What I've done," he says, stepping towards me, "is unlock the vast potential of your mind. You're not just a patient, Abigale. You're the key to revolutionizing human cognition."

His words, spoken with such conviction, momentarily stun me. I struggle to process the twisted logic behind his justification, my mind reeling as I try to comprehend the depths of his delusion.

"You're insane," I whisper, more to myself than to him.

Dr. Harker laughs, a chilling sound that echoes off the stark walls of the chamber. "Insanity is just a label given by those too afraid to push beyond conventional boundaries. What I'm doing here, what I'm doing with you, will change the world."

As he speaks, I feel a surge of something dark and powerful within me, my anger transforming into a force I can barely contain. The surrounding air seems to thicken, charged with an energy I don't fully understand but instinctively know is dangerous.

"You're wrong," I say, my voice gaining strength. "And I won't let you continue this madness."

The fluorescent lights above us flicker and buzz, casting Dr. Harker's face in an eerie, shifting glow. I clench my fists, feeling the rage boiling inside me, threatening to spill over. My voice, no longer quivering, comes out as a low growl.

"You've stolen my life, Dr. Harker. You've twisted my mind and violated my trust. But no more."

I take a step forward, my bare feet cold against the tile floor. The surrounding air begins to shimmer, like heat rising from the pavement on a scorching day.

Dr. Harker's eyes widen, a mixture of fascination and fear playing across his features. "Fascinating," he murmurs, reaching for a nearby clipboard. "The emotional trigger seems to be amplifying your abilities. Tell me, Abigale, what do you feel?"

His clinical tone ignites something primal within me. "What do I feel?" I snarl. "I feel betrayed. I feel used. I feel... powerful."

As the last word leaves my lips, a surge of energy explodes from my core. Papers on nearby desks scatter, equipment rattles, and the lights flicker more violently. Dr. Harker stumbles back, finally showing a hint of genuine fear.

I advance on him, my mind racing. What am I becoming? What has he made me? The questions swirl in my head, but one thing becomes crystal clear—I will not be his experiment any longer.

"Your 'research' ends now," I declare, my voice resonating with an otherworldly timbre. The storm of psychic energy intensifies around me, a visual manifestation of my determination and newfound strength.

Dr. Harker, his back now against the wall, stammers, "Abigale, please. You don't understand the importance-"

I cut him off, my words laced with venomous intent. "No, Doctor. You don't understand. You never did. And now, you never will."

The air crackles with tension as Dr. Harker and I face off, our gazes locked in a battle of wills. My heart pounds, each beat echoing, the surge of power coursing through my veins.

"You've awakened something you can't control, Abigale," Dr. Harker warns, his voice a mix of awe and desperation. "Let me help you harness it. Together, we could revolutionize-"

"Enough!" I scream, my voice reverberating off the asylum's decrepit walls. The fluorescent lights above us shatter, raining glass and plunging us into semi-darkness. "Your 'help' has done nothing but destroy me."

In the dim light, I see Dr. Harker's hand inch towards a nearby syringe. My mind races, recalling countless times he's subdued me with sedatives. Not this time.

With a thought, I send the syringe flying across the room. It shatters against the far wall, the sound oddly satisfying.

"Impressive," Dr. Harker murmurs, his scientific curiosity battling his self-preservation. "But Abigale, you must understand. Everything I've done has been to unlock your potential. To free you from the limitations of your own mind."

I laugh bitterly, the sound harsh and unfamiliar to my own ears. "Free me? You've caged me, experimented on me, treated me like a lab rat. And for what? Your twisted vision of progress?"

As we circle each other in the shadowy room, I feel the weight of every injustice, every violation. The asylum itself seems to groan around us, as if awakening to my pain.

"You're right about one thing, Doctor," I say, my voice low and dangerous. "You have unlocked something. But it's not what you expected. And now, you'll face the consequences."

The storm of psychic energy intensifies, and for the first time, I see real fear in Dr. Harker's eyes. In this moment, I know our fates are inexorably linked, and only one of us will walk away unchanged.

Chapter Twenty-Five

The photograph trembles in my hands, a faded remnant of a lifelong lost. Mother's smile, once warm and comforting, now seems to mock me from behind the cracked glass. Father's stern gaze pierces through time, silently judging the creature I've become. My fingertips trace their faces, willing them to speak, to offer guidance in this labyrinth of madness.

"I won't let you down," I whisper, my voice a ragged whisper in the oppressive silence of my room. "I'll uncover the truth, no matter the cost."

The walls of Crossroads Insane Asylum press in around me, their peeling paint, and mildewed corners a constant reminder of my imprisonment. But I am no longer the frightened girl who first crossed this threshold. I've become something... more.

I close my eyes, shutting out the dismal reality of my surroundings. The darkness behind my eyelid's swirls and shifts, a canvas for the visions that dance at the edge of my consciousness. I reach out with my mind, probing the shadows for answers.

"Show me, Dr. Harker," I murmur, my fingers clenching involuntarily. "Reveal your secrets."

The asylum corridors unfold in my mind's eye, a labyrinth of pain and suffering. I see flashes of Dr. Harker's face, his eyes alight with a fervor that chills me to the bone. His voice, though distant, echoes in my thoughts.

"The human mind is a frontier waiting to be conquered," he says, his words dripping with arrogance. "And I will be its conqueror."

My heart races as I delve deeper, pushing past the barriers of my own fractured psyche. The asylum's history unfurls before me, a tapestry of cruelty and despair. I see Dr. Everett's legacy, the foundation upon which Dr. Harker now builds his twisted empire.

"You're both monsters," I snarl, my teeth clenched against the onslaught of images. "But I'll stop you. I have to."

The visions intensify, threatening to overwhelm me. I grip the edges of my chair, anchoring myself to reality as I navigate the treacherous waters of my own mind. Sweat beads on my brow, a physical manifestation of the mental strain.

"Focus, Abigale," I command myself. "Find the truth. Find the way out."

As suddenly as they began, the visions recede, leaving me gasping in the dim light of my room. The photograph lies forgotten on my lap, a relic of a past that no longer defines me. I open my eyes, my gaze fixed on the door that leads to the asylum maze of horrors.

"I'm coming for you, Dr. Harker," I whisper, my voice steady despite the trembling in my limbs. "Your reign of terror ends now."

The world around me blurs as I'm plunged back into the psychic vortex. Flashes of Dr. Harker's experiments assault my senses, each more horrifying than the last. I see patients strapped to chairs; their eyes wide with terror as electrodes pulse against their temples. The air fills with their agonized screams, a cacophony of suffering that threatens to shatter my resolve.

"No, please!" I cry out, my voice mingling with theirs. "Stop this madness!"

But the visions continue relentlessly. Hidden rooms materialize before me, their walls stained with unspeakable atrocities. In one, I see Dr. Harker hunched over a writhing figure, his scalpel glinting in the harsh fluorescent light.

"The mind is a labyrinth," his voice echoes in my head. "And I am its cartographer."

I try to look away, but I'm helpless against the onslaught of images. My grip on reality begins to slip, the boundaries between past and present, vision and memory, blurring into a nightmarish tapestry.

"Who am I?" I whisper, my sense of self fragmenting. "Where does Abigale end and the asylum begin?"

The walls of my room seem to breathe, pulsating with malevolent energy. I catch glimpses of my reflection in the cracked mirror—sometimes me, sometimes a stranger with wild eyes and a mouth twisted in a silent scream.

"I'm losing myself," I gasp, clutching my head. "Dr. Harker, what have you done to me?"

But even as I struggle against the tide of madness, a part of me knows that this is the key to unraveling the asylum's secrets. I must endure, must push through the chaos to find the truth that lies hidden beneath layers of deception and pain.

"I won't let you win," I growl, focusing on the face of my tormentor. "Your experiments end here, Dr. Harker. I'll make sure of it."

I claw my way back to lucidity, my fingernails digging into my palms. The pain anchors me, a tether to reality amidst the maelstrom of visions. I force myself to breathe, to focus.

"Connect the threads," I mutter, my voice raspy. "See the pattern."

Images flash before my mind's eye: Dr. Everett's cold smile as he injects a screaming patient, Dr. Harker's arrival with boxes of strange equipment, hushed conversations in darkened corridors.

"They're working together," I realize, my heart racing. "But why? What's the endgame?"

I push deeper, ignoring the pounding in my skull. Flashes of blueprints, scribbled notes, and shattered minds coalesce into a horrifying picture.

"They're building something," I whisper, bile rising in my throat. "A machine to... to harvest psychic energy?"

The pieces click into place with sickening clarity. Dr. Everett's cruel experiments weren't just sadism—they were preparation. And Dr. Harker...

"He knew about me all along," I gasp, my chest constricting. "My abilities, my potential. He's been grooming me, pushing me to the brink to amplify my powers."

The truth crashes over me like a tidal wave of ice. Every gentle word, every compassionate gesture—it was all manipulation. I was never a patient to be cured, only a battery to be drained.

"No," I choke out, tears streaming down my face. "I won't let them use me. I won't be their pawn."

But even as I make this vow, a part of me wonders—is it already too late?

My eyes snap open, the visions fading, but their impact seared into my psyche. The room swims into focus, and my gaze locks onto the door leading to Dr. Harker's office. It looms before me, no longer just wood and metal, but a threshold to confront the architect of my torment.

"I can do this," I whisper, my voice trembling. "I have to."

My hands shake as I push myself up from the chair, fingers tracing the worn photograph of my family one last time before I slip it into my pocket. The weight of it grounds me, a reminder of what I'm fighting for.

I take a deep, shuddering breath, willing my racing heart to slow. "Focus, Abigale," I mutter to myself. "You're stronger than they know."

As I approach the door, my reflection catches in its polished nameplate. I barely recognize the gaunt, wild-eyed woman staring back at me. Is this what they've reduced me to?

"No," I growl, clenching my fists. "This is what they've awakened in me."

My hand hovers over the doorknob, trembling with a cocktail of fear and anticipation. The metal feels ice-cold against my skin, sending a shiver down my spine.

"Whatever lies beyond this door," I think, steeling myself, "I'll face it. For every patient they've tortured, for every mind they've shattered. For myself."

With one final, steadying breath, I wrap my fingers around the knob. The moment stretches, taut as a violin string about to snap. Then, with a surge of determination, I twist.

Chapter Twenty-Six

The door creaks open, revealing a dimly lit corridor that stretches before me like the maw of some ancient beast. Flickering fluorescent lights cast grotesque shadows on the peeling wallpaper, each one a twisted reminder of the horrors that have transpired within these walls.

I take my first step into the hallway; the floorboards groaning beneath my weight. The sound echoes through the emptiness, a mournful cry that seems to reverberate through my very bones.

"Keep moving," I whisper to myself, my voice barely audible over the pounding of my heart. "Don't let them see your fear."

As I make my way down the corridor, memories of past torments flash through my mind. The screams of other patients, the cruel laughter of orderlies, the cold touch of Dr. Everett's instruments. Each step is a battle against the urge to turn and flee.

But I press on, my determination growing with each passing moment. The faces of those I've left behind, those who couldn't escape, fuel my resolve.

"I'm coming for you, Dr. Harker," I think, my jaw clenching. "Your reign of terror ends tonight."

The air grows thicker as I approach his office, laden with an almost palpable sense of dread. The door looms before me, a towering monolith of polished oak that seems to pulse with malevolent energy.

I pause, my hand hovering inches from the doorknob. The weight of what lies ahead crashes over me like a tidal wave. Am I ready for this? Can I truly face the monster who's haunted my nightmares?

"You have to be," I remind myself, drawing strength from the depths of my fractured psyche. "For all of us."

With trembling fingers, I reach for the handle, ready to step into the lion's den.

I grasp the cold metal of the doorknob, my fingers trembling as I turn it. The click of the latch echoes like thunder in my ears. I push, and the door swings open with an ominous creak, revealing the sanctum of my tormentor.

The room before me is bathed in shadows, illuminated only by a single desk lamp. Its sickly yellow glow casts grotesque patterns on the walls, were bizarre diagrams and charts loom like spectral observers. The air is thick with the scent of old leather and something metallic—blood?

My eyes lock onto Dr. Harker, seated behind his imposing mahogany desk. His piercing gaze meets mine, a mixture of curiosity and arrogance dancing in those cold, calculating eyes. The silence between us is deafening, broken only by the frantic pounding of my heart.

"Ah, Abigale," he says, his voice smooth as silk yet laced with venom. "To what do I owe this... unexpected pleasure?"

I step forward, willing my legs not to buckle beneath me. "You know why I'm here," I manage to choke out, my voice barely above a whisper.

A smirk plays at the corners of his mouth. "Do I? Perhaps you've come to volunteer for our next round of treatments? Your... unique mind has always been of great interest to me."

His words send a chill down my spine, memories of past "treatments" threatening to overwhelm me. I clench my fists, forcing the images back. "I've already told you... No more treatments," I spit out. "No more experiments. I know what you've been doing—to me, to all of us."

Dr. Harker leans back in his chair, steepling his fingers. "And what, pray tell, do you think you know?"

I open my mouth to respond, but the weight of his gaze makes the words catch in my throat. In this moment, facing the architect of my suffering, I feel small, insignificant. But I can't back down now. The fate of everyone in Crossroads rests on what happens in this room.

I take a deep breath, steadying myself. The room seems to shrink around me, the shadows in the corners growing darker, more menacing. But I press on.

"I know about the secret rooms," I say, my voice growing stronger with each word. "The screams in the night, the patients who disappear. You're not trying to cure us. You're using us. Experimenting on us."

Dr. Harker's eyes narrow, a flicker of something—surprise? anger?—passing across his face. "Fascinating theories, Abigale. But I'm afraid your delusions are getting the better of you again."

"They're not delusions," I snap, taking another step forward. My hands are shaking, but not from fear. Rage courses through me, hot and electric. "I've seen it. The visions... they showed me everything."

A change comes over Dr. Harker then. His mask of calm begins to slip, revealing something darker underneath. "Visions?" he says, leaning forward. "And what exactly did these... visions show you?"

I can feel him probing, searching for weaknesses. But I won't give him the satisfaction. "Everything," I repeat. "Your twisted experiments. The way you've been manipulating us all. Using our pain, our trauma, to further your own agenda."

Dr. Harker stands abruptly, his chair scraping against the floor. The sound makes me flinch, but I hold my ground. "You have no idea what you're talking about," he hisses, his composure cracking further.

I can see the desperation in his eyes now, the anger barely contained. It should terrify me, but instead, it gives me strength. He's afraid. For the first time, Dr. Harker is afraid of what I might know, what I might do.

"Don't I?" I challenge, my voice steady despite the thundering of my heart. "I think I understand perfectly. And it ends now."

I close my eyes, drawing on the swirling maelstrom of psychic energy that churns within me. The room fades away, replaced by a kaleidoscope of horrific visions.

"You see yourself as a visionary," I whisper, my voice echoing with an otherworldly resonance. "But you're nothing more than a butcher."

Dr. Harker's face contorts in shock. "How dare you—"

"I see the truth," I cut him off, my eyes snapping open. They burn with an unearthly blue fire. "The patients you've tortured. The minds you've shattered. All in pursuit of your twisted goal."

Images flood the air between us — spectral projections of Dr. Harker's crimes. Patients strapped to tables, screaming as he cuts into their brains.

Others locked in sensory deprivation chambers, their sanity eroding by the hour.

"Stop this!" he snarls, but I can see the fear in his eyes.

"You wanted to unlock the secrets of the mind," I continue relentlessly. "To push beyond the limits of human consciousness. But you crossed lines that should never be crossed."

My voice rises, filling the room with accusation. "You're not curing anyone. You're destroying them, piece by piece, all to satisfy your own depraved curiosity."

Dr. Harker stumbles backward, his face ashen. "How... how are you doing this?"

I advance on him, my fragile frame suddenly imposing. "You unlocked something in me, doctor. Something you can't control. And now, you'll face the consequences of your actions."

The visions intensify, surrounding us both in a maelstrom of nightmarish memories. Dr. Harker's crimes laid bare, his mask of sanity stripped away to reveal the monster beneath.

Chapter Twenty-Seven

The flickering candlelight casts Dr. Harker's shadow across the worn leather tomes lining his study, a grotesque silhouette that seems to writhe and twist with each guttering flame. I stand in the doorway, my heart pounding a frantic rhythm against my ribcage as I summon every ounce of courage to confront the architect of my torment.

"Dr. Harker," I say, my voice barely above a whisper. "Your reckoning has come."

He turns, his piercing eyes widening in momentary shock before narrowing with calculated precision. "Miss Sheetz," he replies, his tone clipped and cold. "What an unexpected pleasure. To what do I owe this... intrusion?"

I step into the study, the floorboards creaking beneath my feet like the groans of forgotten patients. The scent of musty paper and acrid chemicals assaults my senses, threatening to overwhelm me with memories of countless "treatments" endured within these walls. I push the rising bile back down my throat and force myself to meet his gaze.

"I know what you've done," I declare, my voice gaining strength with each word. "The experiments, the torture, the lives you've destroyed in pursuit of your twisted vision."

Dr. Harker's lips curl into a contemptuous smirk. "My dear girl," he says, his words dripping with condescension, "you speak of things you cannot possibly comprehend. Your fragile mind-"

"My mind is anything but fragile," I interrupt, clenching my fists at my sides. "You've seen to that, haven't you? Years of your 'treatments' have forged it into something far stronger than you ever intended."

A flicker of unease passes across Dr. Harker's face, quickly masked by a veneer of professional detachment. He takes a step towards me, his tall frame looming in the dim light. "Abigale," he says, his voice softening in a way that makes my skin crawl, "you're clearly experiencing a delusional episode. Why don't we discuss this in a more... appropriate setting?"

I stand my ground, even as every instinct screams at me to flee. "No more discussions," I snarl. "No more lies. I'm here for the truth, and I won't leave until I have it."

Dr. Harker's facade cracks, revealing a flash of the predator beneath. "You forget your place, Miss Sheetz," he hisses, all pretense of concern evaporating. "I am the doctor here, and you are nothing more than a troubled patient in need of correction."

His words ignite an inferno of rage within me, fueled by years of helplessness and pain. I take a step forward, my voice low and dangerous. "No, Dr. Harker. You're the one who's forgotten. You've forgotten that even the most downtrodden can rise up. You've forgotten that your actions have consequences."

I see a flicker of uncertainty in his eyes, and for the first time, I realize that the balance of power has shifted. The hunter has become the hunted, and I am no longer prey.

I close my eyes, drawing deep from the well of power within me. The room fades away, and I plunge into the depths of Dr. Harker's mind. A kaleidoscope of memories and emotions assaults me — flashes of cruelty, whispers of forbidden knowledge, and an overwhelming hunger for control.

"What are you doing?" Dr. Harker's voice wavers, panic seeping through his composed exterior. "Stop this at once!"

I ignore his protests, pushing deeper. His thoughts writhe like serpents slithering through dark corridors of consciousness. I see faces—so many faces—contorted in agony, hear screams echoing through sterile halls. My stomach churns as I witness the true extent of his depravity.

"You monster," I whisper, my eyes snapping open. "All those lives... all that suffering..."

Dr. Harker's face contorts, a mix of rage and fear distorting his features. "You have no right!" he snarls, lunging forward. "Get out of my head!"

I sidestep his attack, my newfound strength surprising us both. "I have every right," I retort, my voice steady despite the trembling in my limbs. "You made me what I am, Doctor. Now face the consequences."

He retreats, eyes darting wildly around the room. I can feel his mind racing, searching for a way to regain control. But it's too late. The truth is laid bare, and there's no hiding from it now.

"You don't understand," he pleads, desperation creeping into his voice. "My work is vital. The sacrifices were necessary!"

I shake my head, disgust rising like bile in my throat. "No work is worth that price. No discovery justifies such cruelty."

As Dr. Harker's composure crumbles, I realize that the true horror isn't in what I've seen, but in the knowledge that this is only the beginning of the darkness that awaits me in the depths of Crossroads Asylum.

The flickering candlelight casts grotesque shadows across Dr. Harker's face as I confront him, my voice trembling with a mixture of rage and anguish. "I've seen it all, Doctor. The experiments, the torture, the lives you've destroyed." My fingers curl into fists, nails biting into my palms. "And for what? Your twisted vision of progress?"

Dr. Harker's eyes narrow, a calculated gleam replacing his earlier panic. "Abigale, my dear," he coos, his tone sickeningly sweet, "you're confused. These visions you claim to have... they're merely manifestations of your troubled psyche."

I feel a chill creep up my spine, doubt gnawing at the edges of my mind. No, I think, steeling myself. I know what I saw. "Don't patronize me," I spit. "I've endured your 'treatments' for years. I know the truth."

He takes a step closer, hands spread in a placating gesture. "Your abilities are remarkable, truly. But they're unreliable, tainted by your own fears and traumas." His voice drops to a whisper. "Can you really trust what you think you've seen?"

For a moment, I falter. The weight of uncertainty presses down on me, threatening to crush my resolve. What if he's right? What if I can't trust my own mind?

But then I remember the screams, the pain etched on countless faces. No. This is real. This is the truth he's tried so hard to hide.

"Nice try, Doctor," I say, my voice gaining strength. "But your manipulations won't work on me anymore. I'm not the scared, confused girl you locked away. I'm something else now, something you created but can't control."

Dr. Harker's mask slips, revealing a flicker of genuine fear. And in that moment, I know I have him cornered.

I press forward, my voice rising with each accusation. "You've tortured innocents, Dr. Harker. Twisted minds and broken bodies in your quest for... what? Power? Knowledge? Or just the sick thrill of playing God?"

The flickering candlelight casts grotesque shadows across his face as he retreats, step by step. "You don't understand the complexity of my work," he hisses. "The potential benefits to humanity—"

"Humanity?" I laugh, a harsh, bitter sound that echoes in the dimly lit study. "You've stripped away every shred of humanity from your victims. I've seen the hollow shells you've left behind, doctor. I've heard their silent screams."

Dr. Harker's eyes narrow, a predatory gleam replacing his earlier uncertainty. "And what of your own screams, Abigale? The nightmares that plague you, the voices that whisper in the dark?" His words slither into my mind, probing for weakness. "You're broken, my dear. A shattered mind trying desperately to piece itself together."

I feel the assault on my psyche, his words worming their way into the cracks of my fragile sanity. For a moment, the room seems to warp and twist, reality bending under the weight of his manipulation.

But I plant my feet firmly, grounding myself in the present. "You're right about one thing, doctor," I say, my voice steady despite the trembling in my limbs. "I am broken. But it's that very brokenness that allows me to see the truth. To see you for what you really are."

Chapter Twenty-Eight

I close my eyes, drawing deep from the well of psychic energy within me. The air crackles with unseen power as I reach out, tendrils of my consciousness probing the dark recesses of Dr. Harker's mind.

"No," he gasps, realizing too late what I'm doing. "Get out of my head!"

But it's too late. I plunge into the depths of his memories, unleashing a torrent of repressed horrors. Images flash before us both—patients strapped to chairs, screaming as electricity courses through their bodies; dark operating rooms echoing with muffled sobs; eyes wide with terror as needles pierce delicate skin.

"Stop this!" Dr. Harker roars, clutching his head. But I press on, mercilessly.

"Feel it," I hiss, my voice sounding distant and distorted. "Feel every moment of pain you've inflicted. Every life you've shattered in your twisted pursuit of knowledge."

The candles flicker wildly as Dr. Harker staggers back, colliding with his desk. Papers scatter, fluttering to the floor like broken wings. His carefully cultivated facade of control crumbles, revealing the monster beneath.

"I...I had to," he whimpers, his eyes darting wildly. "For science. For progress."

"For your own ego," I spit back, forcing another wave of memories upon him. The weight of his sins crashes down, crushing his psyche beneath their terrible burden.

Dr. Harker falls to his knees, a broken sob escaping his lips. "What have I done?" he whispers, the truth of his actions finally laid bare before him.

I watch, a mix of satisfaction and horror churning in my gut, as the once-mighty mind's architect unravels before my eyes.

The air in the study grows thick, heavy, as if the very walls are closing in around us. I take a step forward, my bare feet silent on the cold floor. Dr. Harker's hunched form trembles before me, a pitiful sight that stirs no sympathy in my hollowed heart.

"Your 'progress' was built on bones," I say, my voice steady despite the tempest raging within. "But there's one experiment you never accounted for, Dr. Harker. Me."

His head snaps up, eyes wild with a mixture of fear and desperate curiosity. I can see the scientist in him still clinging to life, even as his world crumbles.

"What...what do you mean?" he rasps.

I lean in close, my words a whisper that cuts like a scalpel. "Your ultimate goal. To create a being with unlimited psychic potential. To break the barriers of the human mind."

Dr. Harker's breath catches. I can just about hear the gears turning in his fractured mind.

"You succeeded," I continue, feeling a surge of power course through me. "But not with your machines or your drugs. With your cruelty. Your relentless torture forged something you could never control."

The realization dawns in his eyes, horror blooming like a poisonous flower. "No," he breathes. "It's not possible."

"Isn't it?" I ask, allowing a mirthless smile to curl my lips. "You wanted to play God, Dr. Harker. But you created your own destruction instead."

He scrambles backward, knocking over a candelabra. Shadows dance wildly across the walls as he presses himself against a bookshelf.

"What are you going to do?" he whimpers, all pretense of authority long abandoned.

I consider him for a long moment, feeling the weight of all the lives he's ruined—including my own. "Nothing," I finally reply. "Your own mind will be your punishment. Every moment, every scream, every broken soul...you'll relive it all. Forever."

Dr. Harker's face contorts in anguish as the full impact of my words sinks in. He clutches at his head, a keening wail rising from deep within him. I watch, impassive, as the architect of so much suffering crumples to the floor, lost in the labyrinth of his own twisted psyche.

I turn away from the pathetic figure of Dr. Harker, his sobs fading into the background as I stride towards the door. My fingers brush against the cold brass of the doorknob, and I pause, my heart pounding with a newfound rhythm of purpose.

"This is only the beginning," I whisper to myself, my voice barely audible over the creaking floorboards beneath my feet.

As I step into the dimly lit corridor, the asylum seems to breathe around me. The walls, once confining, now feel like a challenge to be conquered. I run my hand along the peeling wallpaper, feeling the texture of my prison—and my battleground.

My mind races with the enormity of what lies ahead. How many others are trapped here, subject to the whims of madmen like Harker? How deep does the corruption run?

"I'll find you all," I promise the shadows. "Every one of you who thought you could play with our minds, our souls."

A distant scream echoes through the hallway, and a chill runs down my spine. But it's different now. The fear doesn't paralyze me; it fuels me.

I take a deep breath, tasting the musty air tinged with despair. "This place won't break me anymore," I declare, clenching my fists. "I'm coming for you, Crossroads. Your days of darkness are numbered."

With each step, I feel stronger, more determined. The asylum may be a maze of horrors, but I've become something it never expected: a force of vengeance, born from its own cruel experiments.

Behind me, in the study I've left behind, I can almost hear Dr. Harker's mind unraveling. His anguished whimpers fade as I move further away, replaced by the whispers of the asylum's secrets, calling me deeper into its depths.

As I make my way down the corridor, each step a defiant echo against the asylum's silence. My newfound strength courses through me, but the weight of what's to come settles heavy on my shoulders.

"You think you've won, don't you?" Dr. Harker's voice, barely a whisper, slithers into my mind. Even defeated, he clings to his manipulations. "But you've only scratched the surface, Abigale."

I pause, my hand resting on the cold, damp wall. "Get out of my head," I hiss, closing my eyes to focus on pushing him out.

His laughter, tinged with madness, reverberates through my skull. "Oh, but I'm not in your head. You're in mine. You opened this connection, and now you'll see it all."

A flood of images assault me–operating theaters bathed in blood, patients writhing in agony, Dr. Everett's cold eyes gleaming with satisfaction. I gasp, stumbling against the wall.

"Stop it!" I cry out, but the visions keep coming.

"This is what you wanted, isn't it?" Harker's voice drips with venom. "To know the truth? Well, here it is, in all its glorious horror."

I force myself to breathe, to center my thoughts. "You're right," I manage, straightening up. "I want the truth. And I'll use every bit to burn this place to the ground."

The assault on my mind subsides, replaced by a heavy silence. At that moment, I realize the true battle has only just begun. Crossroads Insane Asylum holds secrets darker than I could have imagined, and I've become the key to unlocking them all.

"Bring it on," I whisper in the shadows, a grim smile playing on my lips. "I'm ready for whatever horrors you have in store."

As if in response, a distant door slams shut, the sound echoing through the twisted halls. The asylum seems to draw a collective breath, preparing for the storm that's about to be unleashed within its walls.

Chapter Twenty-Nine

The heavy oak door creaks open, a yawning maw into the belly of the beast. My trembling hand grips the tarnished brass knob as I step into Dr. Harker's shadowy office. The air is thick with the acrid scent of disinfectant and something darker—the cloying stench of secrets long buried.

"Dr. Harker," I say, my voice a wisp of smoke in the gloom. "We need to talk."

He looks up from his desk, eyes glinting like shards of obsidian. "Abigale. To what do I owe this... unexpected visit?"

My heart thunders in my chest, a war drum of fear and fury. I force myself to meet his gaze, to not flinch from the cold calculation I see there. "I know what you've been doing," I whisper, the words clawing their way up my throat. "The experiments, the torture... all of it."

Dr. Harker's lips curl into a cruel facsimile of a smile. "My dear, I'm afraid you're suffering from delusions again. Perhaps we need to adjust your medication."

His dismissal ignites a fire in my belly, burning away the last traces of doubt. I plant my feet, summoning every ounce of strength I've gathered in this house of horrors. "No. I'm not delusional, and I won't let you gaslight me anymore. I've seen the truth with my own eyes."

He rises from his chair, a towering figure of menace and authority. "Abigale, you're a troubled young woman. Your mind plays tricks on you. What you think you've seen—"

"I know what I've seen!" I snarl, my hands clenching into fists at my sides. "The screams in the night, the patients who disappear... You can't hide it anymore."

Dr. Harker's facade cracks for just a moment, a flicker of something dark and hungry passing across his face. But then it's gone, replaced by a mask of patronizing concern. "I assure you, everything we do here is in the name of science and progress. We're working to unlock the secrets of the human mind, to push the boundaries of what's possible."

His words slither through the air, oily and insidious. I feel them trying to worm their way into my brain, to plant seeds of doubt. But I won't let them take root. I can't. The faces of the other patients flash before my eyes—broken, pleading, desperate for someone to believe them.

"You're not a scientist," I hiss, taking a step closer. "You're a monster."

Dr. Harker's eyes narrow, all pretense of kindness evaporating. "Careful, Abigale. You're treading on dangerous ground. Remember where you are, and who holds the power here."

The threat in his voice sends ice through my veins, but I refuse to back down. I've come too far, endured too much. "I'm not afraid of you anymore," I lie, my voice steadier than I feel. "And I won't stop until everyone knows the truth about this place."

As we face each other across the dimly lit office, I can feel the weight of Crossroads pressing down on us both. The asylum holds its breath, waiting to see which of us will break first. And in that moment, I know with terrifying clarity that this confrontation is just the beginning of a war that will consume us all.

My trembling fingers clutch the stack of papers, their edges crumpled from my white-knuckled grip. "You can't deny this," I say, my voice quavering but resolute. I thrust the documents toward Dr. Harker, watching as his eyes narrow behind his wire-rimmed glasses.

"Patient 247, subjected to electroshock therapy without consent. Patient 318, forcibly administered experimental drugs that caused severe psychosis." My voice grows stronger with each accusation. "And here, testimonies from Nurse Wilkins and Orderly Thompson, detailing your late-night 'sessions' with vulnerable patients."

Dr. Harker's facade of calm begins to crack. A muscle twitches in his jaw as he snatches the papers from my hand. "These are nothing but the ramblings of disturbed minds and disgruntled employees," he snarls, but I catch the flicker of fear in his eyes.

"You know they're true," I press on, my heart thundering in my chest. "Just like you know what you've done to me."

He slams the documents down on his desk, the sound echoing through the oppressive silence of his office. "Abigale," he says, his voice taking on a patronizing tone that makes my skin crawl. "You're confused. Your mind is playing tricks on you again. Remember how we've talked about your delusions?"

I feel a flicker of uncertainty, the seeds of doubt he's trying to plant taking root. But I push back against it. "No," I insist, even as memories start to blur and shift. "I know what's real. I remember—"

"Do you?" Dr. Harker interrupts, his voice silky smooth now. "Can you really trust your own perceptions? After all, you're here for a reason, aren't you?"

I falter, my conviction wavering. The walls of his office seem to close in, and for a moment, I'm not sure where reality ends and my nightmares begin. But then I remember the screams echoing through the asylum's halls, the terror in the other patients' eyes. Those can't all be delusions.

Can they?

A sudden wave of clarity washes over me, cutting through the fog of doubt Dr. Harker tries to weave. My spine straightens, and I meet his gaze with newfound resolve. "No," I say, my voice steady despite the trembling in my limbs. "I won't let you twist my mind anymore."

I close my eyes, drawing upon a strength I didn't know I possessed. The surrounding room seems to fade, replaced by vivid flashes of memory—not just mine, but others'. Patients strapped to beds, their screams muffled. Dr. Harker looming over them with a cruel smile. The asylum's dark secrets unfurl before me like a grotesque tapestry.

"I see it all," I whisper, my eyes snapping open. "The experiments, the torture, the lives you've destroyed. You can't hide the truth from me anymore."

Dr. Harker's face contorts with rage and disbelief. "Impossible," he hisses, rising from his chair. "You couldn't possibly—"

"But I do," I interrupt, my voice growing stronger. "I see the darkness in your soul, Dr. Harker. The twisted ambition that drives you to inflict such cruelty."

He stalks around the desk, towering over me. "You have no idea what you're meddling with, Abigale," he snarls, his calm facade crumbling entirely. "I've worked too hard, come too far to let a delusional girl ruin everything."

I stand my ground, even as fear claws at my insides. "I'm not afraid of you anymore," I say, though my voice quavers.

Chapter Thirty

Dr. Harker's hand shoots out, gripping my arm painfully. "You should be," he growls, his face inches from mine. "If you breathe a word of this to anyone, I'll make sure you never see the light of day again. Do you understand?"

I stare into his eyes, seeing the desperation behind his threats. He's scared, I realize. Scared of what I know, of what I could reveal. And that gives me a flicker of hope.

My heart pounds against my ribcage as I wrench my arm free from Dr. Harker's grasp. The room seems to close in around us, the shadows in the corners growing deeper, more menacing. I take a shaky breath, steeling myself for what I must do.

"You can't silence me," I say, my voice barely above a whisper. "Not anymore. I know what you've done to us—to me."

Dr. Harker's eyes narrow. "You know nothing," he spits.

"I know everything," I counter, my words gaining strength. "The experiments, the torture, the... the rape." My voice cracks on the last word, but I force myself to continue. "You tried to impregnate me, didn't you? To create some twisted version of your 'perfect' subject."

His face pales, then flushes with anger. "You have no proof," he snarls.

"I am the proof," I say, my fingernails digging into my palms. "My body, my mind—they bear the scars of your 'research.' And I'm not the only one."

Dr. Harker's composure shatters completely. He lunges forward, grabbing me by the shoulders and slamming me against the wall. "You ungrateful little bitch," he hisses. "After everything I've done for you, this is how you repay me?"

Pain explodes through my back, but I don't flinch. "Done for me?" I laugh, a bitter, broken sound. "You've done nothing but destroy me, piece by piece."

His grip tightens, and I see a terrible gleam in his eyes. "Oh, Abigale," he says, his voice suddenly soft, almost tender. "If you think that was destruction, you have no idea what I'm capable of."

Fear floods my veins, but I can't back down now. I've come too far, endured too much. "Do your worst," I challenge him, even as my mind screams at me to run.

Dr. Harker's lips curl into a cruel smile. "With pleasure," he whispers, and I feel my world begin to crumble around me once more.

The darkness swallows me whole, a pitch-black void that seeps into my very bones. I'm back in my cell—no, not a cell, a cage. The iron bars dig into my skin as I curl into myself, trying to become small enough to disappear. But there's no escape from this nightmare.

"You thought you could challenge me?" Dr. Harker's voice echoes through the emptiness, disembodied and omnipresent. "I am the architect of minds, Abigale. Your pitiful resistance only fuels my resolve."

I squeeze my eyes shut, willing the world away. But behind my eyelids, visions flicker like a broken film reel—fractured memories of experiments, faces contorted in agony, the asylum's dark secrets laid bare. My curse, my gift.

"You can't break me," I whisper, my voice hoarse. "I've seen... I know..."

A cruel laugh reverberates through the air. "Oh, my dear. Breaking you is just the beginning."

Footsteps approach, and I force my eyes open. Dr. Harker looms over me, his face a mask of cold determination. "You've left me no choice, Abigale. Total isolation. No more distractions, no more... influences."

My heart races. "You can't—"

"I can, and I will," he interrupts, his tone matter-of-fact. "Your little rebellions end now. No more contact with other patients, no more staff interaction. Just you, your fractured mind, and me."

Panic claws at my throat. "Please," I beg, hating the weakness in my voice. "Don't do this."

Dr. Harker's expression softens, a mockery of compassion. "It's for your own good, Abigale. You'll see. In time, you'll thank me."

I close my eyes, reaching out with my mind. The asylum groans, as if awakening from a long slumber.

"What are you doing?" Dr. Harker's voice holds a note of panic.

I open my eyes, meeting his gaze. I'm setting us all free.

Chapter Thirty-One

The darkness peels back slowly, like a scab reluctantly giving way to raw, tender flesh beneath. I blink, each movement sending shockwaves of agony through my battered body. The room swims into focus—a windowless tomb of crumbling concrete and rusted metal. My prison. My hell.

I try to push myself upright, but my arms tremble and give out. A whimper escapes my lips before I can stifle it. No. I can't show weakness. Not here. Not now.

The door creaks open, flooding the room with sickly yellow light. A tall figure looms in the doorway, his silhouette etched in shadow. My heart pounds against my rib cage as Dr. Harker steps inside, that all-too-familiar sadistic smile playing across his lips.

"Ah, our little songbird is awake," he purrs, his voice dripping with false sweetness. "Did you sleep well, Abigale? I hope yesterday's...activities... didn't tire you out too much."

Bile rises in my throat. Yesterday. The needles. The electrodes. The screams—were they mine? I can't remember. I don't want to remember.

"Go to hell," I rasp, my voice raw and unfamiliar.

Dr. Harker's smile widens, revealing too-white teeth. "My dear, we're already there. And I'm the devil himself."

He approaches, each step echoing in the cramped room. I shrink back instinctively, hating myself for the involuntary reaction. His eyes gleam with a predatory light as he crouches beside me.

"Such fire," he murmurs, reaching out to brush a strand of hair from my face. I jerk away, ignoring the pain that lances through me. "Even after all this time, you still fight. It's...admirable. Foolish, but admirable."

I glare at him, summoning every ounce of defiance I can muster. "I'll never stop fighting. You can't break me."

But even as the words leave my mouth, doubt gnaws at me. How long have I been here? Days? Weeks? The endless cycle of pain and darkness has blurred time into a meaningless haze.

Dr. Harker chuckles, the sound grating against my nerves. "Oh, Abigale. Don't you see? You're already broken. I'm simply...reshaping the pieces."

His words chill me to my core, but I refuse to let it show. I meet his gaze, unflinching. "You're wrong," I spit. "And one day, I'll make you pay for everything you've done."

For a moment, something flickers in his eyes—surprise? Respect? But it's gone in an instant, replaced by that cold, clinical detachment.

"Bold words from someone who can barely sit up," he muses. "But please — continue to entertain such delusions. They make our brief sessions so much more...interesting."

As he stands, towering over me once more, the weight of hopelessness pressing down. But beneath it, a tiny spark of rebellion still burns. I cling to it, nurturing it with every ounce of strength I have left.

I will survive this. Not only that, but I will escape. And when I do, Dr. Harker will learn the true meaning of pain.

Dr. Harker snaps his fingers, and two burly assistants materialize from the shadows. Their eyes are devoid of empathy. "Restrain her," he commands, his voice dripping with anticipation.

I thrash wildly as they approach, my heart hammering against my rib cage. "No!" I scream, my voice hoarse and raw. Their hands are like vices, gripping my arms and legs. I twist and buck, muscles screaming in protest. For a brief, glorious moment, I wrench my arm free, fingernails raking across one assistant's face.

But it's futile. They overpower me, pinning me down with crushing force. I can't breathe, can't think. The room spins, terror clawing at my insides.

"Impressive, Abigale," Dr. Harker drawls, circling me like a predator. "Your resilience is...fascinating. But ultimately pointless."

He reaches into his coat, producing a device I've never seen before. It's all gleaming metal and wicked edges, pulsing with an eerie blue light. My blood turns to ice.

"What is that?" I whisper, unable to tear my eyes away.

Dr. Harker's lips curve into a cruel smile. "This, my dear, is the culmination of years of research. A device designed to push the human mind beyond its limits. To break through the barriers of consciousness itself."

As he approaches, device in hand, my mind races frantically. There has to be a way out, there must be—PLL.

"You won't get away with this," I hiss, struggling against my restraints. "Someone will find out. Someone will stop you."

He laughs, the sound echoing off the bare walls. "Oh, Abigale. Don't you understand? No one's coming. No one even knows you're here."

The truth of his words hits me like a physical blow. I'm alone. Trapped. At the mercy of a madman.

As Dr. Harker looms over me, device poised, I close my eyes and retreat into the deepest recesses of my mind. Somewhere in this fractured psyche of mine, there must be a way to endure. To survive.

Because I refuse to let this be the end of my story.

The first jolt of pain rips through my body like lightning, every nerve ending set ablaze. I can't hold back the scream that tears from my throat, raw and primal.

"Fascinating," Dr. Harker murmurs, his eyes gleaming with sick fascination. "Your pain threshold is remarkable, Abigale."

"Please," I gasp between waves of agony. "Stop this. I'm begging you."

He adjusts a dial on the device, and the pain intensifies. "Begging won't help you here. This is for the greater good of science."

My world narrows to a pinpoint of excruciating torment. Each second feels like an eternity, my consciousness fragmenting under the assault. I'm dimly aware of my own screams echoing off the walls, a desperate symphony of suffering.

In a moment of clarity between the waves of pain, my eyes dart around the room. There must be something, anything, I can use. That's when I spot it—a loose scalpel on a nearby tray, barely visible in the dim light.

Hope flares in my chest, a fragile ember in the darkness. I gather every ounce of strength left in my battered body and lunge towards it. My fingers brush against cold metal, so close yet so far.

'More,' I think, gritting my teeth against another surge of pain. "Just a little more."

I stretch again, muscles screaming in protest. This time, I won't fail. I can't. My very survival depends on it.

My fingers close around the shard of broken glass, its jagged edge biting into my palm. A surge of adrenaline courses through me, dulling the pain and sharpening my focus. With a swift, desperate motion, I slash at the restraints binding my wrists. The glass cuts deep, blood flowing freely down my arms, but I barely notice. All that matters is freedom.

"What's this?" Dr. Harker's voice cuts through the haze of my determination. "Assistants! Subdue her immediately!"

I hear the rush of footsteps, see the blur of white coats approaching. My heart pounds, a frantic drum in my chest. "No, not again. Never again."

The first assistant reaches for me, and I lash out with the glass. It catches his arm, drawing a red line across his pristine coat. He recoils with a yelp of surprise and pain.

"You won't touch me," I snarl, my voice barely recognizable. Is this really me? This feral, desperate creature? "Stay back!"

Dr. Harker's eyes narrow, a mix of anger and intrigue dancing in their depths. "Fascinating response, Abigale. Your fight-or-flight instincts are remarkably strong."

His clinical tone ignites a new fury within me. How dare he analyze me now, as if I'm still just an experiment? I slash wildly at the air, keeping the assistants at bay. Blood drips from my self-inflicted wounds, each drop a reminder of what I've endured.

"I am not your lab rat," I growl, memories of countless tortures flashing through my mind. "I am not your subject. I am a person, and I will not let you break me!"

As the assistants circle warily, I realize this moment of defiance might be short-lived. But for now, with this shard of glass in my hand, I feel a glimmer of something I thought long-lost in the depths of Crossroads Asylum.

Hope.

I seize my chance. With a primal scream that tears from my throat, I lunge at the nearest assistant. The glass bites deep into his thigh, and he crumples with an agonized howl. Blood spurts, staining my hands crimson.

"Restrain her!" Dr. Harker bellows, but I'm already moving.

My bare feet slap against the cold tile as I bolt for the door. The corridor stretches before me, a labyrinth of shadows and flickering lights. Which way? Left or right? My mind races, fragmented memories of the asylum's layout swirling in a chaotic haze.

"You can't escape, Abigale," Dr. Harker's voice echoes behind me. "This is where you belong."

I choose left, my heart thundering in my chest. The walls seem to close in, whispering secrets of past torments. I shake my head, trying to clear the voices that threaten to overwhelm me.

"No," I pant, pushing myself harder. "I don't belong here. I never did."

The sound of pursuit grows louder. Footsteps, shouts, the metallic jangle of keys. They're coming. My legs burn, muscles screaming in protest after so long confined. But I can't stop. I won't.

I round a corner, nearly losing my balance. A locked door looms ahead. Panic rises in my throat.

"Please," I whisper, rattling the handle desperately. "Please open."

The footsteps draw nearer. I can almost feel their breath on my neck. My fingers, slick with blood, fumble with the glass shard. One last chance...

A glimmer of moonlight catches my eye. There, at the end of the corridor—an open door. Freedom. My heart leaps, hope surging through my veins like a potent drug.

"There she is!" A voice bellows behind me.

I sprint towards the door, my breath coming in ragged gasps. The world narrows to that single point of escape, everything else fading into a blur of shadow and desperation.

"You can't leave, Abigale," Dr. Harker's voice slithers into my mind. "The outside world isn't ready for what you've become."

"Shut up!" I scream, both to the voice in my head and the pursuers at my heels. "You don't control me anymore!"

The door grows closer, tantalizingly within reach. My lungs burn, each breath a struggle. But I can't falter now. Not when I'm so close.

With a last burst of strength, I hurl myself through the doorway. The cool night air hits my face like a slap, shocking my system. For a moment, I'm frozen, overwhelmed by the vastness of the world beyond Crossroads' walls.

"No!" Dr. Harker's anguished cry snaps me back to reality.

I stumble forward, my bare feet sinking into the damp earth. The surrounding woods loom before me, a dark sanctuary offering concealment. My body trembles, weakness threatening to overtake me. But the primal need to survive, to escape, propels me onward.

"Keep running," I whisper to myself, pushing deeper into the forest. "Don't look back. Just keep running."

As he turns to leave, I gather what strength remains. "I'll never break," I call out. "I've seen the truth. The asylum's history, your true nature—it's all here." I tap my temple, a defiant gesture.

He pauses at the door, looking back with a mixture of curiosity and disdain. "And what good is that knowledge if no one will ever hear it?" The door slams shut, leaving me alone with the echoes of his words and the weight of my visions.

The silence engulfs me, suffocating and absolute. I curl into myself on the cold floor, my body a constellation of aches and bruises. The dim light flickers, casting grotesque shadows that seem to writhe and reach for me.

"No," I whisper, squeezing my eyes shut. "Not real. Not real."

I retreat inward, diving deep into the recesses of my mind. The asylum fades away, replaced by a sprawling meadow bathed in golden light. Wildflowers sway in a gentle breeze, their sweet scent a balm to my battered senses.

"This is my sanctuary," I murmur, feeling a spark of hope ignite within me. "He can't touch me here."

But even as I bask in this mental refuge, a part of me remains vigilant. I know Dr. Harker won't give up easily. His voice echoes in my memory, a chilling promise:

"Your mind is a fascinating labyrinth, Abigale. I will map every dark corner, every hidden pathway. And when I'm done, there will be nowhere left for you to hide."

I shudder, the idyllic meadow wavering. No. I must hold on to this. It's all I have left.

A sharp pain lances through my head, yanking me back to reality. Dr. Harker stands over me, a syringe in hand, his eyes gleaming with a mix of frustration and perverse excitement.

"Still resisting, I see," he says, his voice dripping with false concern. "We'll have to try something... stronger."

I try to scramble away, but my limbs won't cooperate. "What are you doing?" I gasp, terror clawing at my insides.

He smiles, the expression devoid of warmth. "Pushing boundaries, my dear. Your resilience is admirable, but ultimately futile. This new compound should prove... enlightening."

As the needle pierces my skin, I cling desperately to the image of my inner sanctuary. But darkness creeps in at the edges, threatening to consume everything.

"Fight it," I tell myself, even as my vision blurs. "Remember who you are. Remember what you've seen."

Dr. Harker's voice fades in and out, a sinister lullaby. "Let go, Abigale. Embrace the void. It's the only way forward."

I feel myself slipping, falling into an abyss of fractured memories and distorted realities. But deep within, a tiny flame of defiance still burns, refusing to be extinguished.

The world spins, a kaleidoscope of nightmares and half-forgotten truths. I cling to that spark of defiance, nurturing it with every ounce of strength I have left. Dr. Harker's face looms before me, distorted and monstrous.

"You can't break me," I spit, my words slurred but resolute. "I've seen... I know what you've done."

He laughs, the sound grating against my frayed nerves. "And who will believe the ravings of a madwoman?"

I force myself to focus, pushing through the haze of drugs and pain. "The truth... always comes out," I manage, my eyes locked on his. "You can't hide forever."

Dr. Harker's smile falters for a moment, a flicker of uncertainty crossing his face. It's enough to fan the flames of my resolve.

"You underestimate me," I continue, each word a struggle. "I'm not just your subject. I'm your reckoning."

He scoffs, but I see the unease in his eyes. "Bold words from someone strapped to a table."

I close my eyes, reaching deep within myself. The visions come, unbidden - flashes of past experiments, faces of those who didn't survive. I channel their pain, their anger, feeling it build within me like a storm.

"You've created something you can't control," I whisper, my voice gaining strength. "And it will be your undoing."

The lights flicker, and for a moment, I swear I see fear in Dr. Harker's eyes.

I blink, and the world shifts. The sterile walls of the examination room dissolve into the shadowy corridors of Crossroads. I'm stumbling, my bare feet slapping against cold tile, each step an agony. But I can't stop. I won't.

"You can run, Abigale, but you can't hide," Dr. Harker's voice echoes, seeming to come from everywhere and nowhere. "This asylum is your home now. Your prison."

I grit my teeth, tasting blood. "No," I rasp, "it's yours."

My fingers trail along the peeling wallpaper as I navigate the twisting hallways. The asylum speaks to me, whispers of long-buried secrets seeping from its very pores. I listen, absorbing every horror, every injustice.

"I hear them," I murmur, my eyes darting to shadows that seem to move of their own accord. "All the souls you've tormented. They're with me."

A cruel laugh rings out. "Your mind is fracturing, my dear. Embrace the madness."

I shake my head violently, strands of matted hair whipping across my face. "You're wrong. I see clearer than ever."

I round a corner and freeze. Dr. Harker stands at the end of the corridor, a silhouette of malevolence.

"It's time to end this game," he says, advancing slowly.

I stand my ground, drawing strength from the very walls around me. "You're right," I say, my voice steady despite the tremors wracking my body. "But not on your terms."

Chapter Thirty-Two

The cold metal bites into my flesh, an icy serpent coiling around my limbs. My heart thunders against my rib cage, a frantic bird trapped in a cage of bone. The basement's stale air presses down on me, heavy with the scent of mildew and something darker—something that reeks of decay and shattered minds.

Shadows dance at the edge of my vision, taunting me with half-formed horrors. I strain against the restraints, feeling them cut deeper with each desperate movement. My breath comes in ragged gasps, echoing off the damp concrete walls of this hellish chamber beneath Crossroads Asylum.

A door creaks open, the sound piercing through the silence. Footsteps approach, measured and deliberate. I know those steps, that rhythm—it haunts my nightmares.

Dr. Harker emerges from the gloom, his silhouette backlit by the sickly glow of flickering fluorescent lights. My body goes rigid, every muscle tensing as if preparing for a blow. His eyes, cold and calculating, lock on mine. A smile spreads across his face, a grotesque parody of warmth that sends ice through my veins.

"Ah, Abigale," he purrs, his voice a silken caress that makes my skin crawl. "How kind of you to join me for our...session?"

I want to scream, to spit defiance in his face, but terror steals my voice. My mind races, fragmented memories of past torments flashing before my eyes. What fresh horror has he devised? What further mutilation of my psyche does he plan?

Dr. Harker approaches, each step bringing him closer to the table where I lie helpless. His presence looms over me, suffocating in its intensity. I can smell antiseptic and something else—a coppery tang that speaks of blood and pain.

"You've been the most fascinating subject," he continues, running a finger along the edge of the table. "But we've only scratched the surface of your potential."

My thoughts whirl in a maelstrom of fear and desperation. I search for an anchor, something to keep me tethered to reality as panic threatens to consume me. But there's nothing here except cold metal, harsh light, and the monster that wears a doctor's face.

Dr. Harker leans in close, his breath hot against my ear. "Shall we begin?" he whispers, and I feel my sanity start to fray at the edges.

I clench my fists, willing strength into my trembling body. The fear is a living thing inside me, writhing and clawing, but I force it down. I won't let him see me break. Not again.

"Why?" I croak, my voice hoarse from disuse. "Why are you doing this to me? What's your endgame, Dr. Harker?"

His eyes glitter with cruel amusement as he straightens, towering over me. "Ah, Abigale. You are always so inquisitive, even in the face of your own destruction. It's one of the things I admire about you."

I watch as he turns, pacing the length of the table. His movements are fluid, predatory. "You see, my dear," he continues, "the human mind is a labyrinth of untapped potential. Most people barely scratch the surface of their cognitive abilities. But you...you're different."

My heart races, each beat a thunderous echo in my ears. What does he mean? What makes me so special in his twisted worldview?

Dr. Harker stops, fixing me with an intense gaze that seems to pierce through to my very core. "Suffering, Abigale, is the key to unlocking that potential. With every experiment, every torment, we push the boundaries of your psyche. We break down the walls that confine your mind, allowing it to expand beyond normal human limitations."

I feel nauseous, his words seeping into me like poison. "You're insane," I whisper, but even as I say it, a part of me wonders if there's a grain of truth in his madness.

He laughs, a chilling sound that reverberates through the basement. "Insanity, genius–the line between them is razor thin. And I intend to obliterate that line completely, with you as my magnum opus."

The metallic clank of instruments being arranged sends shivers down my spine. Dr. Harker's back is turned as he meticulously prepares for what he's dubbed the "last experiment." My mind races, desperately clawing for an escape route.

"You won't get away with this," I say, my voice trembling despite my attempt at defiance. "Someone will find out."

Dr. Harker chuckles, not bothering to face me. "Oh, Abigale. Who would believe the ravings of a madwoman?"

His words ignite a fire within me, memories flooding back of other patients—their haunted eyes, their broken spirits. Sarah, with her perpetual tremors. Marcus, who'd scream for hours about the shadows in his cell. How many had suffered at Harker's hands?

"They weren't all mad when they came here," I spit out. "You made them that way."

He turns, a syringe glinting ominously in his hand. "Perhaps. But their sacrifices paved the way for your ascension."

As he approaches, faces flash before my eyes—not just patients, but staff who looked the other way, families who abandoned their loved ones to this hell. The weight of their suffering, of this asylum's dark legacy, settles on my chest.

"I'll stop you," I vow, straining against my restraints. "I'll expose everything you've done here."

Dr. Harker's lips curl into a cruel smile. "My dear, by the time I'm finished with you, you won't even remember your own name."

The needle plunges into my arm, a searing pain that quickly gives way to an icy chill spreading through my veins. I gasp, my vision blurring as the room begins to spin.

"What...what have you done to me?" I choke out, my tongue feeling thick and foreign in my mouth.

Dr. Harker's face looms above me, his features twisting and morphing in grotesque ways. "I've opened the door to your mind, Abigale. Now, we'll see what crawls out."

The ceiling above me melts away, revealing a starless void. I blink, and suddenly, I'm falling through it, tumbling end over end into nothingness. Panic claws at my throat as I scream, "No! Make it stop!"

But there's no stopping this descent into madness. The void gives way to a kaleidoscope of memories and nightmares. I see the asylum's corridors stretching infinitely before me, lined with doors that bang open and shut of their own accord. From behind them, I hear the wails of countless tortured souls.

"This isn't real," I whisper to myself, squeezing my eyes shut. But when I open them, I'm face to face with my younger self, eyes wide with terror as she's dragged into Crossroads for the first time.

"Help me!" she cries, reaching out. However, as our fingers touch, she crumbles to ash, scattering in a non-existent wind.

I stumble backward, only to collide with something solid. Turning, I stare into Dr. Harker's eyes, now pools of inky darkness.

"Fascinating," his voice echoes from everywhere and nowhere. "Your mind is even more resilient than I'd hoped. Let's see how far we can push it."

Epilogue

The world shifts again, and I'm strapped to that cold metal table once more. But now, the walls of the basement pulse like a living thing, and shadowy figures dance at the edges of my vision.

"Please," I whimper, tears streaming down my face. "I can't take anymore."

Dr. Harker's laughter reverberates through my skull. "Oh, but we've only just begun, my dear. Your fears are the key to unlocking your true potential."

As the shadows creep closer, taking on the forms of my deepest terrors, I realize with horror that this nightmare has no end in sight.

I claw desperately at the fraying edges of my consciousness, trying to anchor myself to something—anything—real. "My name is Abigale Sheetz," I rasp, my voice barely audible over the cacophony of tormented screams echoing through the basement. "I am... I am..."

But who am I? The question splinters my thoughts like shattered glass.

"You are nothing," Dr. Harker's voice slithers into my mind. "Nothing but a vessel for my ambitions."

"No!" I shriek, thrashing against my restraints. The metal table beneath me begins to melt, its surface bubbling and hissing. "I won't let you win. I won't—"

My words dissolve into an agonized wail as liquid fire courses through my veins. My back arches off the table, every muscle seizing in excruciating spasms.

"Fascinating," Dr. Harker murmurs, leaning over me. His face blurs and shifts, becoming a grotesque mask of all my tormentors. "Your mind fights even as your body fails. Tell me, Abigale, what do you see?"

I try to speak, but only a gurgling moan escapes my lips. The basement walls pulse with a sickly, organic rhythm, closing in around us. Shadows writhe and dance, taking on monstrous forms.

"I see..." I gasp, fighting for each breath, "I see the truth of this place. The souls you've destroyed. The lives you've ruined."

Dr. Harker's eyes gleam with a mix of curiosity and cruel satisfaction. "And what will you do with this truth, my dear? You're fading fast."

As another wave of agony wracks my body, I lock eyes with my tormentor. "I'll make sure... everyone knows... what happened here."

My vision begins to darken at the edges, the world narrowing to a pinpoint. But even as my life force ebbs away, I cling to that one final promise—a vow of justice that transcends the boundaries of life and death.

The basement of Crossroads Insane Asylum fades away, and suddenly, I'm standing in a sun-drenched field. The warmth on my skin feels alien after so long in the cold, damp darkness. I see faces—so many faces—emerging from the golden light.

"Mom?" My voice cracks. "Dad?"

They smile, but their eyes are sad. I reach out, but they're just beyond my grasp.

"I'm sorry," I whisper, tears streaming down my cheeks. "I tried to be strong, I tried to—"

A kaleidoscope of memories floods my mind: my first day at the asylum, terrified and alone; the countless "treatments" that left me broken and confused; the fleeting moments of clarity when I realized the true nature of this place.

"No," I rasp, my body convulsing on the cold metal table. "I can't... I won't let them win."

Dr. Harker's voice cuts through the haze. "It's almost over, Abigale. Let go."

But I cling to the faces of those I've lost, to the injustices I've witnessed. "The others," I manage to choke out. "What about... the others?"

"Shh," Dr. Harker soothes, his tone sickeningly gentle. "They're beyond your help now."

I feel my grip on life loosening, my breath coming in shallow gasps. "No," I insist, though my voice is barely audible. "I'll find a way... I'll come back... I'll—"

The words die on my lips as my body goes limp. In that final moment, as my spirit slips free from its earthly prison, I make a silent vow. I will not rest until the truth of Crossroads is revealed, until every tortured soul finds peace.

As darkness claims me, I hear Dr. Harker's last words: "Remarkable to the very end. Sleep now, Abigale. Your fight is over."

But he's wrong. My fight is just beginning.

The basement falls into a deathly silence, broken only by the soft hum of machinery and the steady drip of water from a leaky pipe. My body lies motionless on the table, a shell of the person I once was. Yet, something lingers—an energy, a presence, a whisper of consciousness that refuses to fade.

I can't see, not in the traditional sense, but I perceive. The darkness of the basement seems to pulse and writhe, alive with shadows that dance at the edge of perception. Dr. Harker moves around my lifeless form, his footsteps echoing in the cavernous space.

"Such a waste," he mutters, running a hand through his hair. "So much potential, and now..."

I want to scream, to lash out, to make him understand that I'm still here, but I have no voice, no form. I'm trapped in a liminal space between life and death, aware but powerless.

The weight of my death hangs heavy in the air, a palpable force that seems to press down on everything. Even Dr. Harker, for all his clinical detachment, appears affected. He pauses, staring at my body with a mix of frustration and something that might be regret.

"What secrets did you take with you, Abigale?" he whispers. "What truths lie buried in that brilliant, broken mind of yours?"

If I still had a heart, it would be racing. Even in death, he sees me as nothing more than a subject, an experiment to be dissected and analyzed. The injustice of it all fuels my determination to linger, to find a way to make things right.

As Dr. Harker begins to clean up, preparing to dispose of my body, I focus all my energy on staying present. I won't let the darkness of this basement, of this asylum, swallow me whole. I am more than just a lifeless form on a table. I am memory, I am will, I am vengeance.

And as the last echoes of life fade from this room, I make a silent promise to every soul who has suffered within these walls: This is not the end. It's only the beginning.

Don't miss out!

Visit the website below and you can sign up to receive emails whenever Ashley Marie publishes a new book. There's no charge and no obligation.

https://books2read.com/r/B-A-HVZJC-ITBMF

BOOKS 2 READ

Connecting independent readers to independent writers.

Did you love *Welcome to the Asylum*? Then you should read *Knock Knock*[1] by Ashley Marie!

[2]

On the brink of Lily Simon's eighteenth birthday, a malevolent force from her family's past reemerges to orchestrate a twisted vendetta. Eighteen years prior, the vile Mr. Simon unleashed unimaginable horrors upon young Samara, leaving her spirit forever tormented and marked by the brutality she endured.

As the eerie echoes of Halloween fill the air, Lily becomes an unwilling participant in Samara's grim game. Where each harrowing moment forces her to confront Samara's painful memories in excruciating detail. The chilling "Knock Knock" reverberates through the walls, amplifying the dread that envelops her.

Prepare for a harrowing journey into the abyss of human depravity, where unspeakable terrors lie in wait. This gripping narrative spares no detail, plunging into the darkest corners of the human mind with relentless ferocity.

---

1. https://books2read.com/u/bokLJp
2. https://books2read.com/u/bokLJp

Get ready to have your nerves frayed, and your spirit indelibly marked by the spine-tingling truths that lie ahead.

Also by Ashley Marie

Asylum Duet
Welcome to the Asylum

Bloodline Echoes
Knock Knock
Hide and Seek
Ring Around The Rosy